JULIAN PATI

Frog City and the Racing Frogs

Illustrated by Jon Purkis

Published by Wacky Web Fun
Wacky Web Fun Ltd., Wellington House,
31-34 Waterloo Street, Birmingham, B2 5TJ, England

Wacky Web Fun Ltd., registered offices,
Wellington House, 31-34 Waterloo Street,
Birmingham, B25TJ, England

www.wackywebfun.com

First published 2004
Text copyright ©Julian Patrick, 2004
Graphics copyright © Wacky Web Fun Ltd., 2004
All rights reserved

ISBN 0-9547879-0-0

Printed in Great Britain by
Biddles Ltd. King's Lynn

Contents

This book is dedicated to Teresa – thanks for sticking by me and putting up with my many weird and wacky "projects".

Many thanks to Richard Newbold – the website is amazing

And especial thanks to John Marsden, David Anderson, Peter Orton, Philip Orton, Neil Faulkner, Dave, Carole, Paul, Debbie, Neil, Lynda, Nick and Jane.

Basil – lots of love. We miss your funny ways.

Julian Patrick lives with his girlfriend close to the coast in North Wales. This is his first book.

The Three Toads

The sky is blue and the sun is hot and high. Perched in a tree a blackbird is watching the events on the ground. She can see a small frog dozing on a smooth pebble, close to a shallow stream. A short distance away, approaching the frog from behind, are three large toads.

The blackbird feels the urge to take flight. She ruffles her feathers and prepares her wings. Something is wrong; there is danger on the wind.

It only takes a few minutes for the toads to conduct their business with the frog. They slip a large white bag swiftly over his head, bind his flippers in a rough manner and drag him, struggling, into the woods.

The scene disturbs the blackbird. This is usually such a nice area. She takes flight.

1. Todd's Day Out

This particular day was important to Todd. Today Fat Toad, the famous storyteller, was visiting Frog Pond and Todd was being allowed to travel there alone for the first time.

'You're a little small for your age, but you are growing up fast,' his mother had said the previous evening. 'I think you can make it to the pond and back by yourself.'

Todd hopped away from the cottage.

'Don't lose your glasses,' she shouted down the path. 'That's your last pair.'

'No mother,' said Todd, in a weary voice. He pushed his spectacles firmly onto his face. 'Don't fuss so much.'

Todd and his mother lived on the outskirts of Frog City, at number seven Stone Lane, in a cottage rented from Frog City Council. The cottage had white walls, a bright red front door and a very scruffy thatched roof.

At the first bend in the lane, he stopped and looked back. Frog City dominated the skyline behind the cottage. The huge concrete and glass superscrapers, backed by the deep blue summer sky, glinted in the midday sun. Behind the tall buildings, the pond shimmered and sparkled. A flotilla of small sailing boats played follow-my-leader, zigging and zagging from one side of the pond to the other. Even from this distance, Todd could hear the jet bikes that were leaving the marina. Next season they were to be banned, but today, as they had done all season, they screamed and buzzed across the pond. Love it or hate it, this was the tourist season.

Todd turned to face in the direction of Muddy Bank. For a moment, he thought of turning back. What if he got lost? What if the snakes got him?

'Don't be such a wimp,' he muttered, for nobody's ears but his own, and he hopped off on his way.

It was not long before he arrived at the edge of Boggy Marsh. The marsh was very muddy, very wet and very big. He knew that it would take some time to reach the other side.

No time to waste, he thought, it won't get any smaller by me looking at it.

Hop… hop… hop… hop…

Mud and more mud, he thought, as far as the eye can see.

Hop… hop… hop… hop…

I wonder how many hops it will take to get to the other side?

Hop… hop… hop… hop…

I should start counting.

Five, hop… six, hop… seven, hop… eight, hop…

Between my toes and up my nose, wash me down with a garden hose.

He continued to count, and have mud thoughts, as he hopped across the marsh.

Mud, earth, soil and dirt; it's always brown when it's on your shirt.

Plants need mud and so do worms; a plant just grows and a worm just squirms.

Finally, on the count of three thousand and seventy four, he made it to the other side.

That was tough going, he thought, and I've got to do it all over again on the way back.

Swimming across the stream at the far end of the field was fun. He loved to swim and the only thing better than getting muddy was feeling clean again. His T-shirt and shorts would soon dry in this weather. Feeling suitably refreshed he hopped off in the direction of "Adrian's Wall", a famous Frog Pond landmark.

His father had taken him to the wall when he was younger, but the size of it still took his breath away. Named after the first frog to climb to the very top – the wall stood over four feet and seven inches high – it was recognised as the ultimate climbing challenge.

The drainage pipe, which ran through the wall, was, for Todd, a particularly big challenge, as he had never attempted it alone. He leapt onto a large pebble and rested. Water from the pipe splashed onto the stones in front of him, a dragonfly darted on its business and a tit chirruped in the branches above.

Sometimes you just have to stop and enjoy the moment, he thought. But he did not stop for long and with one perfectly timed leap he was inside the pipe.

The pipe was dark and the small white spot of light at the far end looked a very long way away. He was scared. Some of the older frogs had told him that, at certain times, the ghosts of long dead snakes slithered along the pipe's length. He knew the older frogs were making this up but, for some reason, it did not help very much.

Frogs use this pipe all of the time, he thought, and they always come out of the other end. He gritted his teeth and hopped towards the small circle of light.

Hop, splash, hop, splash...

No such thing as spooks, he thought. His small heart beat fast and hard, and the splashing sounds caused by his hops echoed around and along the walls of the pipe.

Hop, splash, hop, splash...

Lots of frogs use this pipe. I'll be okay.

Hop, splash, hop, splash...

Nothing scares me.

Hop, hop, splash, splash...

The small white circle of light was a little larger now.

No going back, he thought.

Splash, splash, hop, hop...

It can't be <u>much</u> further.

Hop, splash, <u>hissssssssssss</u>...

'What's that noise?' he said, in a rather high-pitched voice. He was not expecting an answer and he certainly did not wish for one.

Hop, splash, hop, splash...

I don't like it in here, he thought.

Hop, splash, hop, splash, hop, splash, <u>slitherrrrrrrr</u>...

'Ribbitt, ribbitt.'

Todd's heart thumped and thudded in his chest, as if at any moment it might burst free, and he started to hop very fast, faster than he had ever hopped in his life.

Hop, splash, hop, splash, hop, splash, hop, splash, hop...

'Aaaaaaaaaaaaaaaaaarghhhhhhh!'

With his eyes closed, he threw himself into the now very large circle of light; he landed with a loud splash in Harriet's Pond (named after Harriet Hislop: the first frog to venture solo through the pipe).

'Pah, easy peasy,' he spluttered, as he surfaced, squinting his eyes against the brightness of the day.

From the exit of the pipe, he was being watched.

'Next time,' hissed a very hungry snake. 'Next time.'

Unaware of his narrow escape Todd swam to the pond's edge, and, using the exposed roots of a small tree, he climbed up the steep bank.

'Handy place to put a tree,' he said to a small vole busy digging a hole under one of the roots. The vole ignored him and continued with his digging.

Suit yourself, thought Todd.

From Harriet's Pond it was not far to his destination, the part of

Frog Pond known as Muddy Bank. This was a mainly grassy area, which would flood following the smallest amount of rain. A large arrow thoughtfully placed at a fork in the path, pointed towards Todd's destination.

"FAT TOAD HERE TODAY," a second sign proclaimed.

Todd made his way down to a small pebble beach, which skirted the water's edge. Leaving home early turned out to have been a very good idea: all of the front-row and most of the second-row pebbles had already been taken. He bagged a smooth, firmly grounded, second row sand-coloured pebble, and sat down.

Not a bad spot, he thought, feeling rather pleased.

A few feet in front of him was a large flat stone; this was obviously reserved for the star attraction. Four glass bottles, each labelled "Frogjuice", stood to one side of the stone and two tall lily plants, lashed by their long stems to two posts, ensured that the stone and the drink were shaded from the hot sun.

Todd spun around on his seat and gazed out across the beach. Young frogs were arriving from all directions; some were alone, but others were with their brothers, sisters or even their complete families. The adult frogs did not sit on the pebbles; they chose, instead, to congregate beneath three large bushes.

The beach filled very quickly and it seemed only a short time before every last pebble was occupied; some bigger pebbles provided seating for two, three or even four frogs. Todd laughed at the sight of a young frog who was desperately trying to stay atop a pebble rather too round to be suitable. He had just decided to try to guess how many frogs were on the beach when there was a huge roar from the crowd around him. He spun around to face the front.

Sitting on the large flat stone was the biggest and fattest toad he had ever seen. A huge mass of brown flesh was topped with eyes twice the size of any frog.

'Wow,' he said to the frog on the pebble next to him. 'Is he scary or what?'

As if to some hidden command the crowd fell silent. The Fat Toad, expanding outwards as he did so, drew a deep breath. His big eyes surveyed the frogs assembled before him.

'Welcome frogs of Frog Pond,' he boomed. 'This is a big crowd today and I am pleased: there are plenty of new minds for me to educate and entertain with my wit and wisdom.' He seemed to be staring straight at Todd, who felt his green cheeks turn a bright shade of pink.

'Everybody calls me the Fat Toad, perhaps because I'm a toad and perhaps because I am very fat.'

The crowd roared with laughter.

'Well, that's fine and dandy with me my little green friends. I have been known as the Fat Toad for so long now that I have forgotten my real name!' His huge, dirty brown bulk shook and wobbled as he laughed and once again, the crowd roared with laughter.

'Silence!'

The crowd fell quiet at the Fat Toad's command. There was not a voice, a ribbitt, nor a whisper to be heard – even the birds ceased their song. Todd dared not breathe, in case he made a sound.

The Fat Toad surveyed the scene in front of him, his big eyes scanning slowly, as if noting each and every frog before him. His audience was spellbound and he was pleased with himself.

'I am going to tell you the story of Frog City.'

His voice had softened a little. A few birds dared to burst into song and a hundred and thirty-seven frogs expelled the air from their lungs.

And the best-known storyteller this side of Frog Pond began his tale.

2. The Frog City Story
(narrated by The Fat Toad)

'There was a time when Frog Pond was a quiet, idyllic, backwater, known only for its clear waters and abundant wildlife. There was not a house or a shop to be seen. This was until a certain young frog arrived in the neighbourhood, a frog who went by the name of Fergal Ribbitt. Many of you will have heard of Fergal. Do not believe everything you hear. A few of the stories are true, but many are not. Rumour and gossip have tarnished Fergal's reputation and it is my job to set the story straight.'

Todd thought he detected a hint of anger in the Fat Toad's voice, and he felt guilty when he thought of the stories he had chosen to believe.

'Fergal arrived at Frog Pond a long time ago, one of the high spirited youngsters visiting the annual Pond Festival of Music. He was a bit of a rascal, a wide-eyed frog with a penchant for mischief, never really fitting in at school and always in trouble for some prank or other. Teaching his classmates how to play Poker, and winning many of their belongings in the process, was the final straw for the school elders, and Fergal was expelled a few days into his final term.'

The Fat Toad shuffled on his stone. His brown fat wobbled and his big eyes blinked.

'But, my little green hoppers, Fergal was not a stupid frog. Even at school it was obvious he was creative, always coming up with some money making scheme. After being thrown out of school, he established his own company. He sold bottled water that, according to the label, was taken from a secret Craggy Hills spring. For a while he was successful, especially after he had a letter printed in the Creek Gazette, which questioned how safe it was for frogs to drink the water from Stumpy Creek – something they had been doing for very many years.

'But Fergal was not behaving at all honestly. His bottled water was not quite what it seemed. Late one night he was observed filling his Craggy Hills bottles in Stumpy Creek. He was forced to come clean. He admitted that the Craggy Hills Spring was a figment of his own imagination and Craggy Hills Pure Spring water was, in fact, common Stumpy Creek water.'

The Fat Toad chuckled.

'What a naughty little rascal Fergal was, selling the Stumpy Creek frogs their very own Stumpy Creek water.

'At his trial Fergal was lucky only to receive a community service order. He spent the next five days clearing rubbish from the east bank of Stumpy Creek.'

The Fat Toad hesitated, his attention diverted by a small insect that had dared to venture within his field of vision. A fraction of a second later, following a flash of pink tongue, the insect was no more. Looking pleased, he continued, 'Fergal never forgot the excitement of running that first business and it was these memories that led him to Frog Pond. He knew there would be many thousands of frogs at the festival and he had over five hundred empty bottles to get rid of. With the help of his friend Eric, and the use of Eric's truck, he set up a small stall manufacturing and selling his new concoction. He called the new drink Frogjuice.'

The Fat Toad took one of the bottles of Frogjuice from the stone.

His huge hands made the bottle appear half the size Todd knew it to be. With two glugs and a wobble of one of his many bellies, the bottle was emptied. He belched and continued his tale.

'The stall consisted of a small wooden shack with a large wooden table out front. A giant lily was suspended over the table, protecting Fergal, Eric and the first bottles of Frogjuice from the sun. Only Fergal was allowed inside the shack and he guarded his secret recipe as if his life depended upon it. If you were to put your ear to the shack's timber walls you might hear the Frogjuice noisily brewing.'

The audience laughed as the Fat Toad attempted a variety of fizzing, glugging and popping noises.

'The festival was the busiest ever and on the first day Fergal and Eric sold over a hundred bottles of Frogjuice. As word about the delicious new drink spread, the queues outside the shack got longer and longer and, in order to keep up with demand, Fergal and Eric worked from dawn until dusk. Production finally ceased half-way through the very last day when the supply of empty bottles was exhausted.'

The Fat Toad glugged another bottle of Frogjuice and, for the second time, he belched out loud. He looked pleased with himself and his big eyes scanned his audience. For a few minutes he said nothing at all. The birds stopped singing and the frogs were completely silent. It seemed to Todd that even time itself had come to a halt.

'Boo!' boomed the Fat Toad.

The frogs in the front row jumped first followed, a fraction of a second later, by the frogs in the second, third and subsequent rows.

The Fat Toad roared with laughter as the ripple of jumping frogs expanded outwards. All six of his bellies came to life, wobbling and bouncing like a stack of joyful jellies. He laughed so hard he nearly fell from his stone and it was a good few minutes before he calmed down enough to speak.

'Please forgive me,' he said chuckling. 'But sometimes I just cannot help myself.'

Todd laughed until he thought his sides might burst. The frogs who had fallen from their pebbles – much to the amusement of those around them – dusted themselves down and returned to their seats.

The Fat Toad, still chuckling and giggling, continued, 'Now I know you are all awake, we can proceed with the next part of the story.

'The festival ended and Frog Pond's visitors soon drifted away. Fergal and Eric stayed behind and, with the proceeds from the sale of the five hundred bottles of Frogjuice, built a new shack. The Frogjuice Factory, as Fergal called it, was three times the size of the first shack. It had a small sales counter at the front and beds for Fergal and Eric at the rear. You can visit this same shack today, preserved forever as a tourist attraction in the Frogjuice Corporation Visitor Centre.' The Fat Toad blinked and sniffed his own armpits. 'Have any of you frogs been to see it?'

About half of the frogs in the audience nodded.

'Sales of Frogjuice grew at an amazing rate. Eric turned out to be a brilliant salesfrog, entertaining shopkeepers with his many stories. His favourite story was about the day the Juicer Mk. 1 expired, blowing itself into a thousand pieces and covering Fergal from head to flipper in Frogjuice.

'It wasn't long before an even larger factory was completed. It was hailed by Frog Global magazine as "the biggest drinks production facility in the world" and had a warehouse, which could despatch two Frogjuice laden trucks every minute of every day.

'Frog Town was also growing fast, with new houses, apartments and shops springing up every week. The Pond Times named Fergal as "Business Frog of the Year" and Frogjuice was named "Product of the Year" by Frog Trader magazine. It seemed to the world that Fergal could do no wrong.'

The Fat Toad drank his third bottle of Frogjuice. This time he did not belch, but he did do something else rather unpleasant. The frogs in the first row pinched their noses.

'But Fergal was in for a rather nasty surprise. The Frog Pond Times printed a front-page story, written by a renowned expert in frog dietary habits. The article discussed concerns that young frogs were drinking too much Frogjuice, and the fact that many were becoming fat, unfit and lethargic. The article conceded the drink was full of vitamins and, in reasonable quantity, was very good for frogs. However, in its conclusion it stated "too many calories and not enough exercise" was harmful to the health of youngsters.

'The article had an immediate effect. Parents stopped their offspring from drinking Frogjuice, many retailers removed bottles from their shelves and there were anti-Frogjuice demonstrations outside of the factory.' The Fat Toad's expression changed to one of sadness. 'Fergal was devastated. For a whole week he locked himself away in his apartment. He refused to talk to anyone about the article – especially the newspapers. Sales of Frogjuice fell dramatically, production lines slowed almost to a halt and the bright-green Frogjuice trucks stood idle in the yards.

'But Fergal was not a frog to be beaten for long. When he finally emerged from his apartment, under his arm was a long cardboard tube. The press surrounded him as soon as he stepped outside, but he refused to speak to them, instead he hopped off down the street. The press gave chase of course, shouting and ribbitting while their cameras flashed and their lenses pointed. Two streets away, outside of the door to the Frogjuice Corporation Headquarters, Fergal stopped. From inside the cardboard tube he extracted a rolled-up poster and he pinned it firmly to the door. Then, refusing to answer any questions, he hopped back to his apartment.'

The Fat Toad reached behind his stone and picked up a cardboard tube. From the tube he extracted a poster; he held it high in order that his audience might see. He looked very proud of himself. 'This is the very poster Fergal pinned to the door on that day.'

Pond Racing Event

On the day following the next full moon
at
Muddy Bank

1st Prize 100 Gold Coins, 2nd Prize 75 Gold Coins,
3rd Prize 60 Gold Coins

ALL FROGS ARE WELCOME

The Frogjuice Corporation is committed to the
health and fitness of all frogs and has pledged the sum of 10,000
Gold Coins. This sum is to be invested in the new sport of Pond
Racing. Part of the investment will be used to establish a
national chain of Fit Frog Centres.

I personally pledge that my mission in life from this day on will
be to make Pond Racing available to all frogs.

Fergal Ribbitt
Chief Executive Officer, Frogjuice Corporation FLC

For the benefit of the frogs at the back, the Fat Toad read aloud from the poster. When he had finished he rolled it up neatly before sliding it back into the tube.

'Well, my little green reptilian friends, the next day's newspapers were full of the story. Everybody wanted to talk about pond racing and every young frog wanted to take part. The newspapers hailed Fergal as a genius and those that had written him off only a few weeks before were now singing his praises.'

A deep frown spread across the Fat Toad's face and he began to rant about the poor behaviour of the press. One of his toad friends coughed in his direction. The Fat Toad scowled, but it did the trick and he continued with the story.

'Fergal and a chosen team of helpers worked hard to make sure that everything was ready for the big day, and he personally designed the first route on which the frogs would race. Other frogs or toads were placed in charge of crowd safety, catering, car parking, toilets, timing and the registration of competitors.

'Assisted by all the free publicity, the first Racing Frogs event was a huge success and, on the day, thousands of frogs visited Muddy Bank. Many came to compete but far more turned up for a good day out.

'The race followed a course that tested competitors to the limit: up hill and down dale, through Bluebell wood, over the stream, across the pond and even through the Muddy Bank pipe. Many competitors, unable to complete the full distance, dropped out of the race due to exhaustion. Of the three hundred and fifty-three frogs that started the race, only seventy-nine crossed the finishing line. The winning frog, a youngster known as Fast Larry, was famous long after the event ended. At an emotional prize giving he received a huge golden cup, one hundred Gold Coins and, best of all…' The Fat Toad chuckled and grunted. 'A kiss from Miranda Slim, Frog Town's 1982 Beauty Frog.

'Fergal must have felt very pleased with himself. Frogjuice sales once again soared to new levels and production lines rattled at full pelt. He kept his word and spent much of the rest of his life establishing the new sport of Pond Racing. Fit Frog Centres were built in every major town, exactly as he had promised. Today, as I am sure you are all aware, frog racing (as it is now called) is a major sport around the world. Frog Pond has grown into one of the best known of all holiday resorts. In the summer the pond is full of tourists and we thank them for the money they spend in our shops, hotels, restaurants and attractions.'

Todd beamed with pride. The place where he lived was famous and it felt good.

'Well, that's the end of today's story. I'll be here with another story soon and I hope to see you all again. Thank you for being such an attentive bunch.'

The audience rose to their flippers and applauded, cheered and ribbitted for all they were worth. The Fat Toad, beaming with pleasure, soaked up the applause, encouraging the crowd by gesturing with his arms for more. The noise seemed to go on forever and was deafening. The Fat Toad loved every minute. He glugged his last bottle of Frogjuice and the front row evacuated swiftly when, for a second time, he produced a most unpleasant smell.

Todd did not leave immediately, but remained seated on his pebble and waited for the crowd to disperse. He listened as a group of young frogs sang happy birthday to one of their party and he laughed when they grabbed the frog by the flippers and threw him, fully clothed, into the pond. He watched the sun's reflection sparkling on the water and saw the clouds, fluffy and white, hurrying on their journey across the blue sky.

'Are you up there somewhere, Dad?' he asked quietly. 'Can you see me?'

Todd did not know where his father was, or even if he was alive. Twenty-eight days ago, twelve days after Todd had changed from tadpole to frog, his father had disappeared. Nobody had seen him since. His father had left the cottage one rainy morning for his job as a

Park Ranger and had never returned home. The last person to see him on that fateful day was one of his work friends.

'He was digging a trench to irrigate some new saplings, by the stream, near Copse Wood,' the friend had informed the police. 'I met him earlier in the day as well. We had a chat inside the hut where he keeps his tools.'

There was of course a search party. Many frogs and toads from Frog City had turned out, but to no avail. Many, though they did not say so in public, thought a snake had taken him.

It goes without saying that Todd and his mother were devastated. It was the not knowing that was the worst.

'What if he's lying somewhere injured, in the woods, with nobody to help him?' his mother had wailed.

'We searched the woods twice over,' a kind police frog had said, 'and the long grass, the pond, the stream and, well everywhere.'

Todd's mother had been ill for many days after the disappearance and Todd had cried himself to sleep almost every night.

Sitting on the pebble, he thought of the events of the last few days. Why can't they leave us alone? Why so soon?

Two days ago, two frogs, both wearing grey business suits and carrying black briefcases, had visited Todd and his mother.

'Mrs Tinpot?' one of the frogs enquired.

'Yes,' his mother replied. 'What do you want?'

The other frog handed Todd's mum a sheet of paper.

'I am sorry to say, that despite numerous reminders, we have received no rent from you for the last twenty-one days. You have seventy-seven days to pay all rent arrears or you must leave the property.'

'But we have no money left,' his mother cried. 'My husband has… well he has…'

But the two frogs were already hopping their way up the path.

What a nightmare, thought Todd. Seventy-seven days to find the money and two days already gone. He was due to start his new job in a few days time, but the small starting wage would barely cover the cost of food.

We owe too much, he thought. Damn the council, damn the snakes and damn everybody!

He looked glumly across to the far end of Muddy Bank where the Fat Toad and his friends were hopping slowly up the beach towards their bicycles.

If I had more time I could start my own business, he thought, just like Fergal did, and Mum and I, we would never be poor again. We could buy a bigger house, have fancy ice creams every day from the Italian place in the city. We could buy our own car and travel to the big Superfrog races and all the frogs would say look, there's Todd in that amazing car and… and…

It was then that the idea came to him – a mad crazy idea – one of those ideas that any normal frog, in any normal circumstances, might think about for only one second before dismissing it from his mind. But these were not normal circumstances, this was serious: Todd and his mother were soon to be made homeless.

It's crazy, but maybe it's possible, he thought, and if it's possible then I should try it. He took a deep breath and, as if it might make the idea sound a little less crazy, he said it aloud: 'In seventy days time there is a Superfrog event at Frog Pond. I have to win it.' Saying it aloud did not help. It was a very crazy idea. The Superfrog competition was the biggest frog race there was, attracting the very best frogs from all over the world. If you stood on a Superfrog podium then you would be very rich indeed. The average age of winning frogs was one hundred and sixty days. Todd was just thirty-four days old and by the time of the Frog City event he would be little more than a hundred days old. He knew nothing about frog racing.

With a huge leap he launched himself from the pebble and set out on his journey home. What a crazy idea, he thought, the craziest idea I have ever had. But his mind was already set.

3. Licence to Hop

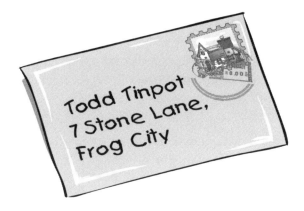

It was a few days after his trip to see the Fat Toad and Todd was sitting hopefully outside of the front of the cottage. He was expecting some post.

At exactly a quarter-to-nine, Larry Stamp, the overweight post-toad, hopped and panted his way up the drive. 'Look's like… something… from Racing Frogs,' puffed Larry, struggling for breath. 'Are you… signing up… for the races?'

'I sure am,' replied Todd as he took the envelope from Larry. 'I'm going to win the Superfrog competition at Frog Pond.'

Todd kicked himself for letting his secret out, but Larry did not appear to take him seriously. 'Your Dad would be proud of you lad,' he said, slapping Todd heartily on the back. 'Best start growing a bit faster, get your mother to feed you up some more.'

'Why is it only frogs that race,' asked Todd. 'Why do you toads not take part?'

Larry laughed. 'We're not built for it,' he said, patting his huge stomach. 'Most toads are a little on the plump side, something to do with our genes I think. Haven't you noticed that toads tend to go for the sitting down jobs? They do enter the races sometimes, but they nearly always do very badly. The committee tried to set up a special toad-racing league, but hardly anybody applied to enter and they gave up. Anyway, got to go.'

Larry wheezed his way up the road and Todd hopped into the cottage. His mother was sitting on a pebble in the corner of the room, knitting something. He ripped open the green envelope. Inside, with his name and picture upon it, was a Racing Frogs' licence. Proudly he showed it to his mother.

'Very impressive,' she said. 'You'd best get out and do some training. It says here that your first race is in three days time.'

'On my way right now,' said Todd. 'I'm off to meet Boris and Cleopatra at the Fit Frog Centre.'

Boris was Todd's best friend. He was five days older than Todd and one of the biggest frogs in the neighbourhood. They had been friends for a while. Boris made Todd laugh because he was always telling jokes and playing the fool. Todd and Boris had met Cleopatra whilst swimming at the posh end of Ribbitt Shallows, outside of the Pink Tongue Hotel. Todd had not been watching where he was going and had knocked into the lily upon which Cleopatra had been sunbathing.

'Watch where you're going you idiot,' she snapped. 'Can't you see anything with those big stupid eyes?'

Todd was extremely embarrassed and, in order to apologise, had hopped onto the lily next to her. He had barely opened his mouth to speak when Boris leapt up beside the both of them. His large frame capsized the lily and plunged all three of them (plus one Frogjuice cocktail and one copy of 'Lover's Leap') into the water. This embarrassing situation had been made even worse by the fact that Cleopatra was not a frog who liked to get wet – a strange trait indeed, for a frog. She had been as furious as it was possible for a frog to be – hopping mad in fact – and it had taken Boris and Todd the better part of the afternoon to cheer her up. Only after her expensive dress had dried, and following three free drinks (courtesy of Todd and Boris), did she eventually see the funny side of the incident. Her friends said later that it was the first time they had ever seen her laugh; she was a rather serious frog. But it all worked out well for the three frogs became the best of friends.

Todd hopped out of the cottage and along the lane to the bus stop. Some fifteen minutes later he was in Frog City, squatting outside of the Fit Frog Centre with Boris and Cleopatra.

Cleopatra was as immaculately dressed as ever in orange "La Frog" t-shirt and baggy "North Shore" surf trousers, which stopped some way above her flippers.

'How was the Fat Toad story?' asked Cleopatra. 'It's a pity we couldn't make it.' Cleopatra had been attending a job interview at the Frog Pond Tourist Information Centre and Boris had been sailing with his dad.

'Brilliant,' said Todd, glancing at Boris. 'I'll tell you about it after the gym.'

Boris seemed a little excitable.

'Ready to get those legs pumping Todd?' he said, hopping up and down on the spot like a mad Jack in the Box. 'No pain, no gain and all that.'

Cleopatra's face showed her displeasure.

'Boris, please stop,' she said. 'It is so embarrassing. He keeps doing it. Can we go inside before somebody has him locked away?'

Todd laughed. Boris had already entered one race and had started training some three days earlier. Cleopatra had no interest in racing. She hated getting wet and, as she put it, "There's too much pushing and shoving".

'You won't have any energy left if you keep that up Boris,' said Todd. 'Come on, let's go.'

The three frogs entered the gym.

4. The Fit Frog Centre

At the reception desk, Todd signed up for full membership, presenting his Racing Frogs licence to a very attractive female frog who was dressed in a pink and silver leotard. After taking his details she smiled and asked Todd if he would like to be shown around.

'No need for that,' said Boris, before Todd had a chance to reply. 'I'll show him the ropes.'

Cleopatra hopped off towards the cafeteria.

Todd and Boris quickly changed into sports shorts and vests. When they entered the gym, Cleopatra, who was watching them from the cafeteria window while enjoying her Frogjuice and Lime cocktail, waved.

The gymnasium was separated into two sections. On the left was a large sign, which read "HOPPING AND LEAPING" and on the right another, which read "SWIMMING". In the hopping and leaping section were six clear plastic tubes, three of which contained a frog engaged in leaping. A sticker on each clear tube read "ACME LEAPING TUBE". Alongside the six tubes were six short conveyor belts, which allowed a frog to hop forwards without actually going anywhere. A sticker on each of these machines read "ACME SPEED

HOPPER". There were just two frogs using these machines. Attached to each piece of equipment was a small computer screen.

'Let's get you in a leaping tube,' said Boris, clearly enjoying showing Todd around. 'After that we'll do some speed hopping.'

Todd, feeling a little apprehensive, nodded.

The clear tube was about ten times taller than Todd and was entered via a round opening at the rear.

'Don't worry, it's quite safe,' said Boris. 'In you get.'

Todd hopped through the hole and into the tube.

'Heard the joke about the frog in a food mixer?' laughed Boris.

Todd stared at him from the inside of the tube. 'Not even a little bit funny,' he said, feeling rather miserable.

Boris laughed again. 'You are squatting on a disc and under the disc there's a spring. In a minute I'll switch the machine on and you need to start hopping. The computer screen will provide information on how many leaps you do, how high you go and how strong your legs are. I have set the machine for three minutes. Okay, start leaping… now!'

The base upon which Todd was squatting suddenly became rather wobbly and he could also feel it vibrating. He started to leap. The spring-assisted surface beneath him ensured he rose much higher than normal.

Boing… boing… boing…

'Five inches! Good work!' shouted Boris. 'Higher, higher!'

'Yeeehaaaaa!' shouted Todd. 'Ribbitt, ribbitt.'

Boing… boing… boing… boing

'Six inches! Go for it!'

Boing… boing… boing… boing… boing… boing

From the cafeteria, Cleopatra saw Todd leaping in the tube and her black pupils bounced in time to his movements.

Boing… boing… boing… boing… boing

'Two minutes to go.'

Boing… boing… boing… boing… boing

'Keep it up,' encouraged Boris. 'Looks like you're getting tired already.'

Boing… boing… boing… boing

'Three inches. You're fading. Ten seconds to go.'

Boing… boing… boing

'Five seconds.'

Boing

'Okay we're done. Out you come.'

Todd hopped out of the tube. Proud of his efforts he turned to smile at Cleopatra, and promptly fell over. His legs seemed to have turned to jelly. Boris and Cleopatra laughed.

'That happened to me,' said Boris. 'You'll get used to it.' He pressed a button on the computer screen and collected the small card that was ejected from its base. 'Your computer card,' he said. 'Not bad – for a first timer.'

Todd, feeling rather embarrassed, staggered to his legs and hopped off to a nearby water fountain for a much-needed drink. This was going to be tougher than he had thought.

'Let's see how fast you are,' said Boris when Todd had recovered. 'Onto the hopping machine.'

Todd followed Boris's instructions and hopped onto the rubber belt of the ACME SPEED HOPPER.

'This machine has six settings,' explained Boris. 'Very slow, slow, medium, fast, very fast and turbo. I'm going to start you on slow, to get the feel of things. Start hopping… now!'

The belt moved beneath Todd's feet and he started to hop.

Hop… hop… hop… hop

'Hey this is easy,' he said. 'Speed it up, Boris.'

Boris pressed the button for the medium setting. The belt started to move a little faster and Todd started to hop a little faster.

Hop… hop… hop… hop… hop… hop

'I could keep this up all day,' said Todd. 'Are you going to get on one, Boris?'

'Who's the new kid?'

The voice came from behind Boris and he turned to see who had spoken.

Four frogs, all in gym wear, were squatting behind him and he recognised one of them at once. It was Sly Spawn, the son of Victor Spawn, a rich and powerful Frog City businessfrog. This was not good. The only stories Boris had heard about Sly and his father were bad ones.

'I said who's the new kid,' said Sly. 'You, the runt on the speed hopper.'

'Leave him alone,' said Boris.

Sly's three bulky friends moved forward a few hops.

'Keep out of it, *Doris,*' said Sly.

'Another time,' said Todd. He avoided looking at Sly who was even bigger than Boris. 'Rather busy at the moment, perhaps catch you another day.'

Before Boris or Todd realised what was happening, Sly reached forward and pressed the Speed Hopper's "turbo" button. The machine seemed to hesitate for a moment, as if not quite believing anybody was daft enough to try this speed. Then, with a high-pitched whistling noise, the rubber mat went into overdrive.

Todd made a valiant attempt at keeping up with the machine, managing six of the fastest hops of his life, but the machine was far too fast and he was thrown across the room, landing with a great splash in the swimming pool.

'Time for a swim,' said Sly. His three friends laughed loudly as the group headed in the direction of the cafeteria.

Todd climbed out of the pool. He was shaking all over. He was angry, upset and confused. He had often been bullied. At school, some of the other frogs had called him stunted, shorty or specky. He had been punched, kicked and spat upon. On one occasion, somebody had put live worms in his gym shoes. It was only after he had met Boris that the bullying stopped. Nobody messed with Boris – nobody until today that was.

Boris and Cleopatra hopped over.

'Sorry Todd, I didn't see him in time,' said Boris. 'That guy is a real idiot.'

'What's his problem?' asked Todd. 'And why would anyone want to hang around with a bully like that?'

'Money,' said Boris. 'His dad, Victor, is really rich. He owns the new holiday resort, which is being built on the edge of Windymore Lake. It said in the paper that it's going to open soon.'

'It's called Las Mega,' chipped in Cleopatra. 'My mum says it could really hurt Frog Pond's tourist industry. I've heard about Victor and Sly. Apparently, Sly gets what he wants, when he wants, with a bucketful of pocket money thrown in. Most of his so called friends are no-brainers, hanging around for free drinks and ice cream.'

'Ah well,' said Todd. 'I had to check out the pool at some stage.'

He smiled, and Boris and Cleopatra laughed. Cleopatra suggested the guys got changed and that they all go down the road to The Green Café for some Dry Roasted Bugs. Todd and Boris agreed.

Deep down, Todd was extremely angry.

5. First Race

It was the morning of Todd's first race and he was out of bed at first light, the only time he had been up before his mother, who was still fast asleep in her bed. He had decided not to tell her about his mad plan to win the Superfrog competition. He wasn't going to tell anybody at all, even Boris and Cleopatra would be kept in the dark. Since the incident at the gym, three days ago, he had trained hard, once a day with Boris and once a day, in secret, on his own. Each evening he had also swum the complete width of the pond, albeit not at the widest point.

He jumped into a pair of green dungarees, put on his favourite white t-shirt, slung his small red rucksack on his back and hopped quietly down the stairs and out of the front door.

Boris was waiting for him by the garden gate. 'Grand morning Todd,' said Boris, looking up at the blue sky above. 'It's going to be a scorcher alright.'

'Let's stop half way for some bugs,' said Todd. 'We're going to need some energy.'

The two frogs hopped off in a southerly direction.

The race was to be held at the southern end of the pond, at Lily

Cove, a small bay famous for being covered almost entirely in water lilies. The journey would take about an hour, just enough of a hop to get warmed up but not so far that they would be tired ahead of the race.

'How's your mum?' asked Boris, as they hopped their way slowly through Snapper Wood.

'Not very good really,' replied Todd. 'She's really sad, never goes out except to get food, just sits at home knitting. I hear her crying sometimes, after I've gone to bed.'

'It must be so hard for the both of you – not knowing and all that.'

'It is. Do you mind if we change the subject?'

The two frogs hopped silently on, along the path and through the wood.

Hop… hop… hop… hop

From the bough of a large Elm tree the blackbird watched as the big frog and the little frog moved slowly through the wood. She had observed the pair since they left the cottage, flitting between their journey and other events of the ground. She watched the beavers building a dam, a snake stalking a small vole, young frogs playing at the edge of the pond and a large rat struggling to climb from the stream onto a slippery bank. From the tree she could see for miles: Frog City to the west, the gathering of frogs at Lily Cove to the south, and Jackdaw Island to the north. It was such a beautiful place that she was unable to prevent herself from bursting into song.

Todd and Boris emerged from the south side of Snapper Wood, where Cleopatra was waiting. Boris hopped towards her, flung himself at her feet and kissed her left flipper.

'We travel these dark and dangerous woods with just a flicker of hope that we might gaze upon your beauty,' he fawned.

'What took you guys?' she asked, looking down at Boris with some alarm. 'You were supposed to be here ten minutes ago.'

'Stopped for breakfast,' said Todd with a grin. 'But Boris isn't very fast when it comes to catching bugs.'

'I am just a simple romantic,' continued Boris, 'unable to concentrate on the tasks of life while such beauty exists at Frog Pond.'

'Todd, this frog's mad,' said Cleopatra, pulling her flipper free. 'Get off my flipper you blubbering idiot. What use is a romantic to me? Do something worthwhile like… invent something or win Superfrog.'

Boris rolled his eyeballs in a full circle then flipped a full backward somersault. The three of them burst out laughing.

'Come on, let's go and race,' said Todd and the three frogs set off towards the cove.

The path that led into Lily Cove was busy with frogs and vehicles: competitors and spectators making their way excitedly toward the race. Cars, trucks, and a number of caravans moved slowly along the middle of the path, whilst Todd, Boris and Cleopatra, and all of those travelling on foot, hopped along its edges. At a fork in the path the vehicles headed left to the vehicle parks and campsite. The frogs on foot headed to the right, towards the race start and to the paths spectators would follow to reach various parts of the course.

The three frogs made their way to the competitors' marquee where Todd and Boris were required to sign in.

'Racing licence please,' said the toad at the entrance to the marquee.

Todd showed his most proudly.

After they had signed in, changed into their shorts and t-shirts and put their bags for safekeeping they met up with Cleopatra.

The start arena was not easy to miss. A huge white banner, the word 'START' printed upon it, was stretched high and tight between two tall saplings. Todd began to feel quite nervous, a little sick even.

'Don't worry,' said Boris. 'First race nerves, happens to us all.'

From the far side of a patch of tall nettles a noise had been increasing for some time. The frogs assembled by the start were all a little curious. The noise – a rhythmic, thumping and whumping with a hint of whining sort of sound – got louder and louder and many of the frogs covered their ears. The tops of the nettles began to sway, slightly at first then rather more so, until they thrashed around in quite a dangerous manner. One young frog, who moved from the area with insufficient haste, narrowly escaped the stinging of his life. A bright, lime-green frogcopter appeared over the agitated plants. It moved slowly over the start arena, causing a terrific wind, which knocked a number of frogs off of their flippers. Very slowly the frogcopter descended into a fenced off area to one side of the marquee, onto a red painted "F". When it was firmly grounded, the engines were cut. The thumping, whumping and whining decreased and the rotor blades slowed until, eventually, they stopped completely. All eyes were on the small door of the now quiet frogcopter. It opened; a frog hopped out. It was Sly Spawn.

'Wow,' said Todd. 'That's one way to make an entrance.'

'I want a helicopter,' said Cleopatra, her eyes positively sparkling. 'Get one for me Boris.'

'I'll order three,' said Boris.

Sly, all eyes upon him, hopped into the competitors' marquee. The pilot, a toad in a smart black suit, extracted a cooler box and a small bag from the helicopter's luggage compartment and then followed Sly.

'Ten minutes until the race starts,' boomed a toad with a megaphone, startling many of the frogs. 'Will all frogs who are not competing leave the competitor's arena and make their way to the spectator areas.'

Before heading off to watch the race Cleopatra kissed both Todd and Boris on the cheek and wished them luck. Todd blushed a bright pink and Boris did a full backwards somersault.

'Two minutes until the race starts,' boomed the toad.

'Remember,' said Boris to Todd. 'Take it easy to start with, or you'll never make it all the way.'

'Okay big guy,' said Todd.

He glanced towards a toad who was sitting on a rock to one side of the banner. The toad wore a bright orange vest with the word 'MARSHALL' printed across its front. In his left hand was a short fat pistol and he was staring at a stopwatch in his right hand. He raised the pistol in the air. A silence descended on Lily Cove. Todd's heart beat fast in his chest.

The pistol fired and the race was on.

Fifty-four frogs had registered for the race. At the sound of the gun they bounded between the two saplings and hopped frantically down the slope leading to the first turning point: a right turn marked by a bright-green circle pinned to the foot of a large Oak tree. Opposite the tree was a stream; the gap between the tree and the stream was wide enough for ten frogs at most. First-corners in frog racing are often eventful and a small group of spectators, including Cleopatra, had assembled by the tree. As the competitors approached, Todd was in the middle of the pack; Boris was already some distance ahead of him. The first twenty or so frogs made it through the gap without incident, but the middle of the pack were not going to be so lucky: too many frogs and too small a gap.

Todd saw the gap was too small and, remembering what Boris had said, he slowed a little. Better to get through in one piece, he thought, and save some energy for the rest of the race.

'Out of the way runt,' said an angry voice from behind. Todd felt a huge push in the middle of his back. Unable to help himself he crashed into the frog in front, who crashed into the frog in front of him and before Todd realised what had happened he was floundering in a pile of green bodies and flippers. Two or three frogs slid into the stream and another cried out in pain as his flipper twisted beneath him. Todd rolled down the bank towards the stream. Luckily his descent was halted by a clump of grass. In the distance he saw Sly, hopping down the path towards the lead pack.

Most of the frogs that had fallen, including Todd, were soon back on their flippers and back in the race. The frog with the injured flipper was unable to continue and was helped to the first-aid tent by race officials. Todd was not pleased about being pushed from behind and hopped along feeling quite angry.

After the first corner, a long path led to the cove and the water's edge. At the end of the path was the pond; it was covered in floating water lilies. He leapt from the bank onto a stable looking lily, then leapt onto another, and another, and another. Each jump was different. A short hop here, a long hop there and, every so often, a giant gap tested his leaping limit. Each lily felt different. Some were steady and this made launching and landing a straightforward process. Others were unstable, tilting or even capsizing if he did not launch or land from their direct centres. Twice Todd ended up in the water and on both occasions he lost valuable time, causing him to be overtaken by more experienced competitors. On the far bank he stopped for a rest. Ahead of him was a very steep slope and he could see the leaders already approaching the summit.

Look at those guys go, he thought, I'll never be that fast.

He set off up the hill.

Hop… hop… hop… hop…

He was tired now and his thighs were beginning to hurt, but he was not doing badly for his first race and he was pleased to pass three other competitors on the way up the slope. It was not long before he found himself squatting on the summit.

'Downhill now,' he gasped.

The rest of the race passed without incident. On the way down the slope he was overtaken once, but he did manage to pass two frogs in the section through the wood and he passed another two frogs on the final swim across the cove. When he hopped his way across the finish line he was utterly exhausted.

6. The Frogjuice Factory

It was Todd's first day at work, as a trainee in the Despatch department of the Frogjuice Factory. He wanted to work in Quality Control, but all new employees were required to start at the bottom and work their way up.

From the cottage, the hop to the factory did not take more than twenty minutes and he was soon standing in front of one of four entrances. The factory consisted of a group of buildings all enclosed within a tall, red-brick security wall. The wall formed a perfect square around the complex and on each of the four sides there was an entrance. On the north-facing wall was the North Entrance; on the west-facing wall was the West Entrance, and so on. Each of the four entrances had been created in the shape of a giant bottle of Frogjuice; these were also constructed in red brick. Through the middle of each of the entrance bottles there was an arch, and above each arch, in big capital green letters, was the word "FROGJUICE".

Todd approached the small guard hut, which was placed slightly in front of and to the right of the East Entrance. Inside the hut was a huge toad, dressed in the Frogjuice security uniform of black shorts, black roll neck jumper and a green cloth beret. The beret was embroidered with a black letter "F". This particular guard was wedged so tightly into his hut that Todd wondered how he might ever get out again. Extending horizontally from the guard hut was a red and white striped security barrier that prevented unauthorised vehicular access.

'It's my first day at work,' said Todd to the toad. 'I was told to report to the Despatch department.'

The toad gave him a long stare before replying: 'Through the arch, across the road and it's the red door straight ahead of you. It says Despatch on the door, if you can read.'

Todd thanked him and ventured through the arch. Without looking left or right, he hopped onto the factory's internal road. A bright green Frogjuice truck braked sharply to avoid him; the driver honked angrily, shaking his fists in Todd's direction.

'And mind the traffic,' shouted the toad from his hut.

Embarrassed at his own stupidity, Todd leaped quickly across the road. He opened the red door and hopped through.

He found himself inside a small rectangular room; the walls and ceiling were painted a brilliant white. The wall, opposite the door through which he had entered was dominated almost entirely by a window, which was obscured by horizontal grey blinds – in the closed position. A frog, with very white hair and wearing a white coat, squatted behind a computer terminal. He looked at Todd.

'Our new little worker I presume. Welcome to Despatch. Please take a seat.'

He pointed to a row of plastic pebbles to Todd's left.

'I'll be with you in about five minutes.'

There was not much to observe in the small white room and while he waited, Todd's thoughts turned to the racing. Fifty days to go until Superfrog, and three races, Lily cove, Muddy Bank and Toad Alley, now completed. Toad Alley had been particularly exciting. The race had started at exactly eleven in the morning and, for the umpteenth time, Todd replayed it in his mind.

Twenty-four frogs had entered the race and only one did not turn up. Sly and his three mates were a part of the lead pack right from the start, pushing and shoving their way to the front of the arena. One unfortunate competitor was injured even before the starting pistol: one of Sly's mates dead-legged him for daring to jostle Sly. Todd stayed well clear.

From the start arena, outside of the Town Hall, the competitors hopped their way along the High Street, turning right onto Spindler's Lane as they left town. They then proceeded along Sapper Straight, a hundred metres of nothing but flat grass with the occasional small bush. At the far end of Sapper's (its nickname), they raced into The Copse, a small wood where Todd found the exposed tree roots very difficult work. Out of Copse and they arrived at the stream where they were presented with a number of options.

They could jump across the stream where it narrowed, above Viagra Falls. This was not the route to take if the stream was running high. It was quite a leap and there was a possibility of falling short and landing in the water. For most frogs a journey over the falls did not bear thinking about.

The second option, chosen by most competitors if the stream was high, was to travel upstream and cross at Fallow Log, a fallen tree that formed a perfect bridge.

The third option was to travel downstream, some twenty metres below the falls. Here the channel narrowed considerably and a frog could cross with even the poorest of leaps. This option was known as Yellow Belly Leap and was, by far, the longest of the three routes.

In this race the choice had been easy. The stream was running low and Todd, like most competitors, jumped the stream above the falls.

From the stream, the competitors headed towards a huge boulder known as Meteor Rock. Todd passed along its right face, the most direct route to the end of the course. It was heavy going here, as the ground was little more than marsh. Once clear of the rock competitors soon arrived at Sandy Beach, a strip of sand running between the pond and the rest of the land. This final stretch really sorted out the fit from the not so fit. Hopping in sand is extremely hard work and this was a very wide strip of sand. Todd had really struggled and was overtaken by at least five competitors as he hopped slowly across.

Twenty-ninth position, he thought. How can I ever be fast enough? I need a top three finish just to qualify to enter Superfrog.

'Are you still with us young Mr. Tinpot?' asked the frog with the white hair. Todd snapped back into reality, into the white room with the big window with the blinds in the closed position.

The frog introduced himself as Smith Green, Smithy for short, and manager of the Despatch department. He informed Todd that he had worked in Despatch since the plant opened, over three hundred days ago. He was proud to have once shaken hands with Fergal himself.

'Of course the old codger's dead now,' he said. 'Probably up to mischief in another world.' For a moment he looked a little sad.

Todd thought of his father and wondered if he was in this other world, with Fergal perhaps.

'I suppose we had better get you started,' said Smithy, reaching across and pulling the string that opened the blinds. He also pulled a small lever, causing the large glass window to swing open. The small room, which had previously been very peaceful, filled with noise.

'Crikey!' said Todd in amazement. 'Take a look at that!'

On the other side of the window was a rectangular room, the size and shape of a large field. To Todd's left, at the far end of the room, two conveyor belts emerged side by side from a large circular hole in the wall. One of the two belts carried row after row of bright green opaque bottles, whilst the other transported a continuous row of red plastic crates. The belts hummed loudly as they travelled the entire length of the room, disappearing empty through another large circular hole, at the far right of the building.

Along the length of the conveyors, at regularly spaced intervals, were six large mechanical arms. At the end of each arm there were what looked like a dozen small claws.

Todd's eyes fixated on one of these machines. The arm swooped down, pistons on its numerous joints pumping and hissing with every movement. The twelve claws grabbed twelve bottles and inserted them neatly into one of the crates. The arm swung back and the whole cycle repeated itself, again and again.

Downstream of each mechanical arm, four frogs stacked the red crates into perfect cubes – twelve crates high and twelve crates wide.

Along the back wall and behind each of the mechanical arms, were six large openings, through which daylight streamed into the building. Every minute or so, the rear end of a green Frogjuice-truck would appear through one of the openings. A frog-operated forklift truck would collect one of the neat red cubes and deposit it into the truck, which would rev its engine before driving away. Each time a truck revved its engine one of the crate stackers would shout 'FROGJUICE AWAY!' at the top of his voice. In response, every other frog in the room would shout 'YEEHAA!' followed by a swift 'RIBBITT!' The truck would move away and daylight would once more stream through the vacant opening.

The factory was as organised as it could possibly be; there was a place for everything and everything was in its place. Yellow paths painted on the white floor showed where a frog could walk and red stripes indicated areas where a frog might be in danger. There were, for example, plenty of red stripes around the mechanical arms.

Smithy saw the astonished expression on Todd's face and he smiled. 'It's the biggest Despatch department in the whole of the frog world. It never stops, night or day. From this department we can fill a truck with Frogjuice every two minutes, if we whack it up to full speed that is. It does happen as well, when we have a really hot spell.'

'Crikey,' said Todd, still amazed.

'That gets 'em all sweating out there,' said Smithy with a chuckle.

He pointed to the hole in the left wall, where the conveyors entered the room.

'The conveyors bring the bottles from the bottling department next door, six bottles in a row. At the maximum speed we can bring twelve bottles per second into this room.'

'YEEHAA!' shouted Smithy, as another truck pulled away from one of the openings. 'RIBBITT!'

'Does everybody have to do that when a truck leaves?' asked Todd, a giggle stirring deep inside his belly.

'Why, of course,' said Smithy, as if Todd had asked a really stupid question. 'It might seem a little strange at first, but everybody gets used to it. It really does add a bit of fun to working here. Every department has its own strange little ways.'

'What's happening over there?' asked Todd, pointing to four frogs standing close to where the conveyors entered the room. 'They are snaffling your Frogjuice for themselves, so they are.'

'Well, let's go take a look,' said Smithy, hopping to the door, which led to the factory floor. 'Follow me and mind you keep to the path.'

Todd followed Smithy, hopping along a yellow path until they came to the four frogs that Todd had mentioned.

'Best job in the factory,' said Smithy. 'Every five-hundredth bottle is selected and tested to ensure it is just the way it should be. There are twelve tasters altogether, working in shifts, especially selected for their strong taste buds and sense of colour and smell.'

The four frogs were assembled around a small wooden table on which were a red plastic bucket and a small chrome rack. Standing vertically in the rack were four large, clear test tubes. One of the four frogs picked a bottle of Frogjuice from the conveyor, unscrewed the silver top and poured an equal amount into the four tubes. The four frogs each picked one of the tubes and, in exact synchronisation, held them up in the air.

'Colour good,' said each frog one after the other and, still synchronised, they lifted the tubes and poured a small amount of the green liquid into their mouths. They did not drink the liquid; they swilled it noisily around their mouths then spat it into the bucket.

Each gave their verdict.

'Juicy Lucy likes it fruity!'
'Juicy Lucy likes it fruity!'
'Juicy Lucy likes it fruity!'
'Juicy Lucy likes it fruity!'
Todd laughed.

'What's *that* all about?'

'The phrase means the Frogjuice tastes just perfect,' said Smithy, before turning to one of the four tasters. 'And what do we say if the Frogjuice is not perfect?'

'Silly Sally likes it sour,' said the taster in a whisper. 'It pains me just to say it.'

'That phrase means there is something wrong with it,' continued Smithy. 'Sally was one of the trainees in the early days. Hopeless she was; couldn't tell vinegar from lemonade that one. But Lucy, now Lucy was our first ever taster and she was good, damn good. The phrases just sort of grew from nowhere but we like to keep them.'

'What happens if the Frogjuice does have something wrong with it?' asked Todd.

'If that happens then one of the tasting frogs sounds an alarm and the whole Frogjuice factory grinds to a halt,' said Smithy. 'Then the Hit Squad goes in.'

'What's the Hit Squad?'

'Twelve frogs, all especially trained to find faults and on call twenty-four hours a day. Anyway, enough chat for now, we need to get you to work.'

Todd spent the rest of his first day at work loading red crates into perfect squares. This he would be doing for thirty days, only then could he apply for work in another department. He would work four hours a day for five days a week. He was pleased to be on the morning shift as this meant he could train with Boris in the afternoons.

By the end of his first day he was quite exhausted. He still made it to the gym though.

7. Training, Racing, Training, Racing

Working at the factory ensured Todd and his mother could buy food and pay at least some of the weekly bills. However, it was not enough to pay the rent and Todd knew the day that they would have to leave the cottage was drawing slowly closer. He had tried to talk to his mother about it, but she did not seem to want to go there.

'Mum, if you got a job then we might be able to save the house,' he said one day, in his most cheerful voice.

'I haven't worked for a long, long time,' she replied. 'Anyway, I need to look after the house for your father. He'll be home soon; he'll know what to do.'

When Todd had tried to explain that his dad might not be coming home, she had become very angry, scalding Todd for having no faith and for upsetting her. He soon learned not to talk about his dad or the possible eviction. The slightest wrong word from him and his mother would fly into a rage.

'She's behaving very strangely,' he told Boris and Cleopatra over a Frogjuice at The Green Cafe. 'Every day she cleans the cottage from top to bottom, sometimes twice, and she sings while she's doing it, like she hasn't got a care in the world. She lays the table for all three of us. Yesterday she even put food on Dad's favourite plate.'

'Sounds like she needs some help,' said Boris, 'or she'll end up in the funny farm.'

Todd did not see Cleopatra kick Boris, under the table.

'It gets worse,' continued Todd. 'When the food was still there after we had both finished, she asked the empty chair if it was feeling okay. She's bonkers, totally bonkers.'

He did not tell Boris or Cleopatra that he and his mother might soon be evicted; his mother had made him promise not to tell a soul. He did however tell them about what he had been up to earlier that same morning.

'Before I came here,' he said, 'I went to Dad's tool shed at Lily Springs. The shed is a right mess. Burglars broke in the day after Dad went missing; they wrecked the place.'

'They want their flippers chopping off,' said Cleopatra angrily.

'Anyway I remembered he had a secret hiding place, underneath one of the floorboards. It's where he kept his binoculars; he used them to keep an eye out for forest fires. I found the binoculars, but I also found something else.'

Todd looked at Boris and then at Cleopatra.

'Spare us the drama,' Boris sighed impatiently. 'What did you find?'

'I found this.' Todd handed a tattered piece of paper to Boris. 'It's a hand drawn map of a very big house with a huge swimming pool.'

'That's got to be Victor's mansion,' said Cleopatra. 'His place is close to Lily Springs and I heard that it has a pool. It's got a high wall all around it, and guards and spotlights and snakes, which are loose in the grounds – to scare people off. Look, there's a wall on the map.'

'Uurrgh, snakes,' shuddered Boris.

'Why would your dad have a map of Sly's dad's house?' asked Boris.

'I don't know,' said Todd. 'But if it is Victor's house then it's very strange.'

It was indeed a mystery. The three frogs would probably have discussed the matter further, but they had tickets for the cinema and this was one experience they did not want to miss. The film was called 'PIKE', about a huge killer fish terrorising holidaymakers at a busy tourist resort. The poster outside of the cinema promised "a chilling experience".

After the film had ended, the three frogs went to Pizza Plaza, where they ordered hot and spicy bug pizzas and, of course, Frogjuice.

'That was one scary film,' said Todd.

'Especially when the Pike attacked the boat,' said Boris. 'I nearly puked when that frog had its flippers bitten off.'

'The Pike did look a bit rubbery sometimes,' said Cleopatra. 'And what was that woman wearing on the beach; those clothes were so yesterday.'

'Cleo, you're a typical female,' said Boris. 'Some woman's kids are being slaughtered by a Pike and you're looking at what she's wearing.'

'I had to watch something,' said Cleo. 'I had my eyes closed for most of the film.'

'Dare you go back into the water?' said Boris, mimicking the voice from the advertising for the film. The three of them laughed but all agreed that swimming in the pond would never feel quite the same again.

Todd and Boris visited the gym together every day after work and on most days they managed a swim across the pond and back. Boris had recently passed his *big-truck* driving test and had started work as a driver for the Frogjuice Corporation.

On many days Cleopatra came to watch them at the gym. She was quite a busy frog herself, training to be a massage and beauty therapist. This caused Boris a great deal of amusement and not a day would go past without him making some kind of comment.

'Practice on me,' he would beg, on one occasion lying almost naked across Cleopatra's kitchen table. 'My thigh, my thigh, oh it hurts so much, just a little rub Cleo, just a light caress from your tender green fingers.'

Cleopatra was having none of it and she told him to take a cold shower.

Todd's performance on the hopping and leaping machines improved each time he visited the gym. He had saved all of the computer cards and had them pinned onto a wooden board in his bedroom. But it was swimming he was particularly good at and this had not gone unnoticed at the gym.

'You're a natural in the water,' said the top coach at the Fit Frog Centre. 'It helps with you being small; you have less drag. It's a shame you can't see where you're going half the time.'

Todd wasn't allowed to wear his glasses in the pool and more than once he had inadvertently changed lanes and crashed into some frog or other. Unfortunately for him, one of these frogs had been Sly, and Todd had spent the next few days with a black eye. Sly had said that it was Todd's own fault, for not looking where he was going. He also said that Todd had 'swum into his fist', was a 'specky loser' and that Sly was going to 'thrash him' in the races.

If the training was tough then competition in the races was even tougher and Todd was finding it hard to make the progress that he wished for. He had improved his performance in all of the last three races: he finished twenty-fourth position at Lily Cove, twenty-second at Muddy Bank and a very respectable sixteenth position at Toad Alley. It was here that he had, for the first time, finished ahead of Boris. He had also finished ahead of Sly.

'Thrashed him,' he said to Boris. That had made them laugh for a long time.

8. Cleopatra Has an Idea

Both Boris and Cleopatra were furious when they found out who was responsible for Todd's black eye.

'It's about time we sorted this Sly out, once and for all,' said Boris. 'He seems to have it in for Todd.'

'Why do you think he doesn't like me?' asked Todd.

'It's not worth wasting energy thinking about,' said Cleopatra. 'He's a bully and he picks on those smaller or less strong than he is, it's that simple. Anyway, I've found out some more about him.'

Todd and Boris looked at her.

'Come on then,' said Boris. 'Spill the beans.'

'Well, when I found out about Todd's eye last night, before I met up with you guys, I went to see Sally, a friend of mine. She works at "Bug U Like", one of Victor's companies; they own those stalls which sell hot bug baguettes at the races.'

'Spicy Cockroach with a barbecue sauce, you can't beat it,' said Boris, licking his lips and stroking his belly.

'Shut up Boris,' said Cleopatra.

'Apparently Sly's dad, Victor, is a bit of a workaholic. He leaves home at dawn and is rarely home before dark; that's if he makes it home at all, especially now Plas Mega is about to open.'

'Where exactly is Plas Mega?' asked Todd.

'Windymore Lake, the nearest pond to ours,' said Cleopatra. 'It's about an hour away by car. We should go for a day trip sometime.'

'I heard that Las Mega has the biggest hotel in the world,' said Boris. 'It said in the newspaper that Victor is allowing jet bikes as well, and that the hire place has a full fleet of the new Mosquito R5's.'

'He should be ashamed of himself,' said Cleopatra. 'Jet bikes are noisy and smelly and it's only frogs with small brains that ride them.'

'I like them,' said Boris defensively.

'I rest my case,' said Cleopatra sharply.

'Look, can you two get back to the point,' said Todd.

Cleopatra continued, 'Victor has three apartments in Frog City and the mansion in Lily Springs, which is not far from the Chuggi shop, where I get my hats from, and that's where Sly lives.'

'What, in the Chuggi shop?' laughed Boris.

'No you fool, in the mansion.'

'Sly's mother left home shortly after spawning,' said Cleopatra. 'Couldn't put up with her husband always being at work. So Sly gets brought up by a whole stack of nannies and, because Victor feels guilty about not spending time with his son, he spoils him rotten, you know, buys him all the latest toys, gadgets and stuff. Rumour has it that Sly got that helicopter because he was to start work. He said it was too far to hop.'

'Lazy brat,' said Boris.

'Where does Sly work?' asked Todd, half not wanting to hear the answer.

'Good news and bad news,' said Cleopatra. 'The bad news is that he's working for The Frogjuice Corporation. Apparently, his dad pulled a few strings and he went straight in as a trainee manager. There was no period on the factory floor for that guy.'

'All frogs are equal but some are more equal than others,' said Boris, showing off.

'Well that's just great,' said Todd. 'What's the good news?'

'The building where he works is not in the Frogjuice Factory complex but in some posh office in the city, near Frog City Bank.'

'It's not what you know but who you know,' said Todd.

'Anyway,' continued Cleopatra, 'Sally says that Sly always has everything his way and he doesn't like it when he doesn't get what he wants. She also says that he's a bully, but I think we know that already.'

'Is that it?' asked Boris.

'One last thing, you'll like this one; Sly is scared of spiders.'

Both Todd and Boris found this most amusing.

'You've got to be kidding,' said Boris. 'Who has ever heard of a frog that's scared of spiders?'

'Crikey,' said Todd. 'Who'd have thought it?'

'So that gave me an idea,' said Cleopatra, with a rather wicked glint in her eyes. 'I think it's about time we got our own back on Sly.'

Todd and Boris listened carefully to Cleopatra's idea. When she had finished speaking Boris did a double backward somersault, as usual landing perfectly on his flippers.

'Brilliant!' he exclaimed excitedly. 'Absolutely brilliant! When can we do it?'

'I suggest we do it tomorrow,' said Cleopatra, 'during the race at Ribbitt Shallows. It will mean you guys not taking part in the race, but it should be worth it. What do you think Todd?'

Todd's first thought was that he did not want to miss a race, but this was quickly overshadowed by the urge to teach Sly a lesson. He rubbed his black eye and nodded. 'Count me in,' he said. 'Tomorrow it is. But there's something I want to do this afternoon and I want you guys to come with me. I want to go check out Victor's mansion. There has to be some reason that Dad had the map.'

'Sounds fun to me,' said Boris.

'As long as we can visit the Chuggi shop while we're there,' said Cleopatra.

It took the three frogs about an hour to hop to Lily Springs. As on the map, and as Cleopatra had suggested, a huge wall surrounded Victor's mansion. It was far too high for any frog to climb.

'How are we going to see inside?' asked Boris.

'I've already thought about that,' said Todd. 'Dad must have been able to see over the wall in order to draw this map. If you look over there, by those reeds, you can see a wooden lookout tower; the park rangers use it for fire watch. I bet you, that was where he was when he drew the map. I've brought his binoculars. Come on, let's go climb the tower.'

From the top of the tower the three frogs could indeed see over the wall but it was rather a long way away. Todd peered through the binoculars.

'What can you see?' said Boris impatiently. 'Is it bigger than your cottage?'

Cleopatra told Boris that he wasn't funny.

'Nothing too exciting,' said Todd. 'But the house is absolutely massive, there must be fifty rooms in it. There's a big garden, tennis courts and… crikey me… the biggest swimming pool you've ever seen.'

Boris, unable to contain his excitement any longer, snatched the binoculars from Todd.

'You're not joking,' he said. 'And look, there's Sly's helicopter and… and… a jet bike! Wow! It's a Mosquito R4 twin turbo; that Sly is one lucky frog.'

Cleopatra was next to use the binoculars. She was more impressed by the size of the pool than any of Sly's big toys.

'One day I will have a pool that big,' she said, 'and a Gold Card for the Chuggi shop. Hey, there's a lorry delivering loads of boxes to a big door at the back of the house.'

'What's in the boxes?' said Boris hopping up and down impatiently.

'How should I know,' snapped Cleopatra. 'Stop bouncing up and down so I can see properly.'

'FISH FOOD,' she said at last. 'The boxes say "FISH FOOD" on them.'

Todd laughed out loud.

'Sly's dad feeds him on fish food,' he laughed. 'No wonder he's turned out a bit strange!'

This amused the three frogs so much that they struggled to climb safely down from the tower. They continued to laugh all the way home.

That night as he lay in bed, Todd twisted and turned. What did Victor want with a lorry full of fish food? Why did his own dad have a map of Victor's mansion? Had his dad been watching the mansion from the tower? Did any of this have anything to do with his disappearance?

9. The Diversion

The next afternoon, after Todd and Boris finished work, the three frogs arrived bright and early at the Ribbitt Shallows course, a full hour before the race was due to start. There was hardly anybody about, although they did see a group of frogs erecting a marquee at the start arena.

'Okay,' said Cleopatra. 'We need to get Sly on his own. It's no good if his bodyguard mates are with him. What I reckon is this: Sly is fast, often a top ten finisher. Luckily for us his mates are not so quick and towards the end of the race he will likely have left them far behind. We need to think of somewhere we can intercept him.'

'How about Six Trees?' suggested Todd, referring to a group of Sycamores situated some ten metres or so from the route the racing frogs would take.

'Sounds good to me,' said Cleopatra.

'And me,' said Boris.

The three frogs hopped off in the direction of Six Trees.

Ribbitt Shallows is different to the other courses in that it consists almost entirely of swimming. From the start, competitors proceed along a path, a hundred or so metres in length, that weaves through a flat area of grassland before joining another path, this one running along the water's edge and passing Six Trees on its route. Then the competitors enter the water, swimming across the pond, around Jackdaw Island and back again via the same route – the finish being at the same point as the start.

At Six Trees, Todd, Boris and Cleopatra were about to launch their cunning plan.

'Okay,' said Cleopatra. 'I reckon the leaders will be here in about five minutes. Are you all set Boris?'

'Yup,' replied Boris, hiding behind the trunk of one of the six Sycamores. 'This'll teach him.'

'And you Todd?'

'Ready and eager,' replied Todd.

He was only a short distance away from Boris and was hiding in a clump of grass next to the path along which the racing frogs would approach. Sunk firmly into the ground next to him was a sign, a white post with a square of white board at its top. If you were heading along the path you would see only the back of the sign, which was complete-ly blank. On the other side of the sign, the side that the racing frogs would not be able to see unless Todd spun it round, were five words freshly painted by Todd that very morning.

'Right,' said Cleopatra. 'I'm going to hide with Boris. Todd, when you see Sly, you know what to do.' She hid herself next to Boris.

A few minutes later the first of the frogs could be seen in the distance. Will Whistle, (Billy Whiz to his friends) hopped along the path at some speed; he was closely followed by two of his rivals.

He's certainly fast, thought Todd; it will be difficult to beat that one.

The three frogs hopped past Todd, who was well hidden. All of them ignored the sign – the side that they could see was blank. In the distance, a fourth frog came into view. He was on his own; it was Sly. Todd spun the sign around so that the message faced towards the path and, with his heart beating hard, he tucked in small amongst the grass.

Hop… hop… hop…

Todd's heart beat so fast and so loud, he feared that he might be discovered.

Hop… hop… hop…

The hopping stopped and, for a moment, everything except Todd's heart was silent.

'D-I-VERS-ION,' said Sly slowly, reading from the sign before him. 'ALL-FROGS-THIS-WAY.'

Todd had painted an arrow on the sign and this was pointing towards Six Trees.

Then Sly did something Todd had not expected. He pulled the sign from the ground and threw it into the long grass, just behind Todd. For a moment Todd thought that their plan was not going to work.

'Now everybody behind me will go the old way,' laughed Sly, hopping towards Six Trees to where Boris and Cleopatra were hiding.

'Well,' thought Todd, 'that saved me the job of hiding the sign.'

In a clearing, under the tree where Boris and Cleopatra were hiding, was a second sign. Sly frowned, but he hopped towards it.

'ALL-FROGS-READ-THIS,' he said aloud slowly.

'Directly above Sly, tied by its handle to an overhanging branch, was a large plastic bucket. Inside the bucket, and unable to climb out due to its smooth sides, were forty-seven of the biggest spiders that Todd, Boris and Cleopatra had collected earlier that morning.

Sly squinted his eyes and moved closer to the sign. There was some small writing, below the larger writing that he had just read. 'TIME-TO-LOOK-UP' said Sly slowly. 'What the-'

He looked up.

Boris's timing was just perfect. One pull of the long string and the bucket tipped completely upside-down. The forty-seven spiders, some of which were quite huge, rained down upon Sly. 'Like a spider shower,' Todd had later joked.

Well, Todd had not known what to expect, but Sly's reaction was quite amazing. For a few seconds he just froze, his whole body locked as rigid as the frog statues at Frog City Hall. Most of the spiders bounced off him, landing in the grass and scuttling away, pleased to be out of the smooth bucket. Two or three dropped inside Sly's t-shirt, and a little fellow spun a swift line from his shorts to the ground. One of the spiders, an especially large furry-footed beast, landed on his forehead, scrabbling to get a grip on his head. It was probably this particular spider that caused what happened next: Sly started to shake; his leg twitched, his arms trembled and he whimpered. One could see that something was about to happen, and happen it certainly did. Sly flipped out completely: full backward and forward somersaults, side leaps, front leaps, back leaps and rolls in every direction. Throughout these activities he squealed loudly, a most distressing noise, which reminded Todd of a stuck pig. In less than a minute Sly had ripped off his t-shirt and shorts and, dressed only in his underpants, was hopping home, shaking and blubbering like a baby.

'Shocking,' said Boris emerging from his hiding place, 'quite shocking.'

'Nice underpants,' laughed Cleopatra. 'Oh if only we had brought a camera.'

Todd hopped over to join them.

'Double backward somersaults Boris,' he said. 'I thought only you could do those.'

The three frogs sat in the clearing laughing and joking until they thought their sides would burst.

'D-I-VER-SION,' mimicked Boris.

'His face when he looked up,' cried Cleopatra, with tears of laughter in her eyes.

It had been a good day, thought Todd, although he did wonder if they had not gone a little too far. He loved to laugh, but somehow it did not feel quite right while his dad was missing.

It was while they were all busy laughing that one of Sly's mates hopped along the path close by. He wondered what all the noise was about; he also wondered why Todd and Boris were not racing.

10. The Trouble with Frogjuice

It was four days after the incident with the spiders and Todd, Boris and Cleopatra had seen nothing of Sly. He had not been at yesterday's race and they had not seen him at the gym.

Todd had enjoyed yesterday's Muddy Bank race; he had finished in seventeenth position. Qualifying for Superfrog was looking like an impossible goal. He needed a top three place in at least one race and there were only twenty-four days and seven more races to go.

He quite enjoyed his job at the factory and he had made many new friends. Stacking crates was hard work but it provided rewards that he had not thought of: this was extra training and he was definitely getting fitter. At lunchtimes he usually met Boris in the workers' canteen.

'So why do you think Victor took delivery of a lorry-load of fish food?' asked Todd, as they queued for food.

'He's probably into tropical fish. Knowing him, he's probably got a tank the size of a room or something. Anyway, what's it matter? Perhaps he's just a bit weird.'

'We still don't know why my dad had a map of the mansion. Perhaps we'll never know.

Since the visit to see the mansion, Todd had hardly stopped thinking about why his Dad might have hidden the map. Even after their recent visit he was none the wiser. He decided to change the subject.

'What made you to want to work at the Frogjuice Factory Boris?'

'Just love Frogjuice so much. I heard that you could drink as much as you like if you worked here; it sounded good to me.'

Todd laughed. Frogjuice was indeed free for the workers – but only in the canteen, and employees were not allowed to drink it anywhere else in the factory.

The two frogs chose their food, filled their glasses and sat down at one of the many tables.

'Have you seen any of the rest of the factory?' asked Todd.

'Not yet, it's huge. I wouldn't know where to start.'

Todd told Boris about the four main departments within the complex (he had got this information from Smithy, who seemed to know everything about the factory). 'The Storage Facility is where the raw materials are stored. The Juicing Room is where the stuff's actually made. The Bottling Plant, that's where it gets put into bottles, and, of course, there's Despatch, where I work.'

'And the Head Office is in Frog City,' said Boris, crunching through the shell of a toasted cockroach. 'My mum's just started working there, as a secretary I think.'

'I wouldn't mind looking at the Juicing Room,' said Todd. 'I've heard that it's pretty cool.'

Boris looked at his watch. 'We've got half an hour. Let's go see if we can see inside, I know where it is.'

The two frogs left the canteen and proceeded along one of the complex's internal roads. Everywhere there was activity of some description: trucks delivering, trucks collecting and frogs hopping about in all directions.

'Down here,' said Boris, turning left at a junction. 'I think it's that big square building up ahead.'

The building ahead of them was by far the biggest building in the complex. It was constructed entirely of red brick and was different from almost every other building in the complex: it did not have a single window.

The two frogs stopped at a door.

'Employees only,' said Todd, reading from a notice fixed to the door.

'I think this is the *side* of the building,' said Boris. He tried the door but it was locked. 'I thought that there might be a window we could look through. It looks like there's pretty secret stuff in there.'

'Ah well,' said Todd. 'It was worth a try. We can't get in round the front. Smithy says that you need a permit.'

The two frogs turned away and started to hop back towards the canteen.

'Wait,' said Boris. 'Look.'

A frog in orange overalls was hopping towards the door. From her pocket she took a small piece of plastic and, arriving at the door, held it against a small red dot, close to the handle. There was a sharp 'clunk', the door swung open and she hopped inside.

'Quick,' said Boris. 'Go for it.'

Without thinking, Todd hopped after Boris. They only just made it through the door before it shut.

'Crikey!' said Todd, his eyes widening.

'Wow,' said Boris. 'Look at that!'

They were standing on a metal gantry, about half way up the inside wall of the biggest room that Todd had ever seen or ever imagined. The building had looked huge from the outside, but what they had not previously known was that more than half of it was sunk into the ground, making it twice as big on the inside as it looked from the outside.

'Wow,' said Boris a second time. 'It looks like something from a James Pond film.'

In the middle of the room, stretching from floor to ceiling, there was a huge golden sphere. Across the sphere, metre-high green lettering read "Juicer Mk. 27". Six clear pipes entered the sphere at various points around its base, and the whole contraption took the shape of a giant spider. In each of the clear pipes, and travelling into the sphere, was a coloured liquid; there was a different colour in each pipe. These coloured liquids were being drawn from six smaller spheres, each about a sixth the size of the main sphere. The sounds coming forth from the contraption were amazing. It slurped, sucked, boiled, belched and popped like the belly of some suffering beast.

On one side of the sphere, quite high up, was another tube. It was much wider in diameter than the others and carried a bright green liquid the length of the room, before it disappeared through a hole in the wall. Into the bottling department, thought Todd.

'Look at all that Frogjuice,' exclaimed Boris. 'I think I've found heaven.'

'What do you two think you're doing?' said a loud and angry voice.

Todd and Boris turned around. A short distance behind them was a rather huge toad. He was dressed in a Frogjuice Factory security uniform and carried a long wooden truncheon. He hopped angrily towards them.

'Despatch frogs, in the Juicing Room!' he shouted, incredulously. 'You'll have me fired if anybody sees you in here! Let's be 'avin you! Out that door and on your way before we're all in the deep stuff!'

Todd and Boris hopped along the gantry, almost falling through the door in their desire to escape from the toad. They hopped quickly back to the canteen, laughing along the way but still overawed at the room they had just seen.

The rest of the day was uneventful. The bottles and crates moved continuously along the conveyors. The mechanical arms put the bottles into crates and Todd and his new friends stacked the crates into large cubes for the forklift truck drivers, who loaded the crates onto the trucks.

'FROGJUICE AWAY!' shouted Todd as the last truck of his shift departed. 'RIBBITT!'

The whistle for the end of morning shift sounded at midday and he grabbed his small red rucksack and hopped off towards the checking out machine. He was due to meet Boris for training; they had planned a really intense session. It was also pay day, and he wanted to stop and buy his mum some flowers.

He clocked off and headed out of the building – along the internal road that led to the East Entrance. As he hopped through the arch, he waved to Big George, the guard in the hut who had given him directions on his first day. Big George did not wave back.

Two security toads stopped Todd as soon as he left the complex.

'Todd Tinpot,' said the first, grabbing him by the arm. 'Please come with us.'

'What for?' said Todd. 'I've got to get to the flower shop and…'

'Just come this way; it won't take long,' said the second guard. The two toads led Todd back into the complex, across the internal road and into Smithy's office.

Todd's first thought was that he was in trouble because of sneaking in to see the Juicer; he wasn't prepared for what came next.

'Todd,' said Smithy, 'we've had an anonymous report that you were seen putting two bottles of Frogjuice into your bag earlier today. I'm sure there has been a mistake, but would you mind if we take a look?'

'Of course not,' said Todd, feeling slightly bewildered.

He took his rucksack from his back and dropped it clumsily onto Smithy's desk. It clinked loudly.

Todd stared at his bag in disbelief. Smithy opened it and one by one he extracted two bottles of Frogjuice.

'I… I didn't… I didn't put them there,' stammered Todd.

Smithy and the two security guards stared at him. Todd felt his skin reddening and a bead of sweat trickled down his forehead.

'Honestly… I know nothing about them.'

'I am very disappointed in you,' said Smithy, choosing to ignore Todd's protestations. 'The least you could have done would have been to own up.'

'But I…' He did not finish his sentence; he really did not know what to say.

Smithy informed Todd that he would be suspended from work until the next weekly management meeting, in seven days time. At the meeting he would be given five minutes to present his side of the story. Unless he could prove he had not stolen the Frogjuice he would lose his job.

And that was it. Todd was escorted from the Frogjuice complex by the two toad security guards. Outside of the entrance they informed him that he would not be allowed back onto the premises until the day of the meeting.

He hopped slowly home. He was devastated. Of course he had not taken the Frogjuice. He had never stolen anything in his life. But how did it get into his bag? Somebody must have planted it, but whom?

When he arrived home he did not tell his mother about the suspension: she had enough to worry about.

'I skipped the gym,' he said. 'I decided to have a rest day.'

'That's a good idea,' said his mother. 'Perhaps you can help your dad, down by the woods.'

Todd felt like shaking her. He wanted to say that his dad was not down at the woods at all and he was probably dead. But he did not, choosing instead to go to his room; he hopped onto his bed and fell fast asleep.

11. Todd's Choice

Todd stayed in bed all afternoon, all night and all of the next day; he told his mother that he was feeling unwell. He was depressed. There was a race at Lily Cove but he had no stomach for it.

'Oh dear,' his mother said. 'You keep warm in bed. I'll get your dad to pop to the chemists when he gets in from work.'

When Todd looked into her eyes; they appeared dull and listless.

'The lights are on but nobody's home,' he told Boris and Cleopatra, the following day. He also told them about the Frogjuice incident.

'What, they just threw you off the premises?' asked Boris, angrily.

'That's terrible,' said Cleopatra.

The three frogs discussed, at length, who might have planted the bottles in Todd's bag.

'I bet you Sly had something to do with it,' said Boris, 'or one of his gang. Hang about a minute.'

Using his mobile phone, Boris phoned his mother. Todd and Cleopatra heard Boris ask his mother about Sly's whereabouts the previous day.

'Mum's on her lunch break,' he said, when he had finished. 'Apparently, Sly was in his office all day yesterday. However, she did say that he went out for a little while in the afternoon for a hospital appointment.'

'That would have been enough time,' said Cleopatra. 'He could have sneaked in while nobody was watching. Wait till I see him. He'll really need a hospital. I'm going to give him a piece of my mind.'

Todd told her to calm down. 'We don't know it's him. I'm sure it's a good possibility, but you shouldn't presume anything without the facts.'

'We could check out whether he did indeed go the hospital,' said Cleopatra. 'That's if they would tell us of course.'

'I doubt it,' said Todd wearily. 'Anyway, that doesn't prove he did it. He could just say he went somewhere else. It might not have been Sly, we just don't know. I need to think of something to say at this meeting though.'

The three frogs racked their brains until they could rack no more, but couldn't think of anything that would help Todd at the meeting.

'I'll just have to tell the truth,' said Todd. 'What will be will be.' He felt very miserable.

Later that afternoon Boris and Todd went to the gym. Boris had said that it would do Todd good, clear his head and help him to think. He trained harder than he had ever trained before, spending twenty minutes in the Leaping Tube, twenty minutes on the Speed Hopper and twenty minutes in the pool. By the end of the session he was exhausted. It did help though; the picture was suddenly very clear: he would soon have no job and no home. He had to win Superfrog.

The next day's race was at Ribbitt Shallows. Todd arrived early, meeting Boris and Cleopatra close to the start arena.

'Hey Todd,' said Boris. 'How's it going?'

'What a silly phrase,' said Cleopatra.

'About as well as can be expected,' said Todd. 'I'm just trying to concentrate on the race.'

'They're trying out some cameras,' said Boris. 'Testing them ready for Superfrog. Apparently Frog TV are going to put the race out live.'

Todd looked in the direction where Boris was pointing. On top of a long pole a camera moved slowly from left to right, scanning the assembled competitors, many of whom were leaping and waving as the camera pointed in their direction. At the foot of the pole a frog worked a small joystick and watched a computer screen.

'That's a great idea,' said Todd. 'They've got cameras like that in the Frogjuice Factory, you know, for security.'

Even before he had finished the sentence he realised the significance of what he had just said. His eyes opened wide.

'Cameras!' he shouted. 'In the factory. Why didn't I think of that before?'

With hardly a hesitation he turned and hopped away from the arena.

'Todd!' shouted Boris. 'You'll miss the start!'

'Stuff the race! I'll meet you afterwards!'

It took him nearly an hour to reach the factory. Fat George was in his hut and the red and white striped barrier was in the down position. Todd did not care; he hopped clear over the barrier, through the arch and towards the door to Smithy's office.

'Hey!' shouted George, squeezing himself out of the door at the rear of the hut. 'You can't do that!'

You just try and stop me, thought Todd, and he burst through the red door and into Smithy's office.

'What the…!' exclaimed Smithy. 'Oh, it's you.'

Fat George bounded into the office and grabbed Todd from behind. 'Sorry Smithy, he was too fast. Got him now though.'

'Smithy,' cried Todd struggling to break free from Fat George, 'the cameras, they're all over the factory. I need to know if there is one in the locker rooms.'

Fat George was dragging Todd through the door and out onto the road.

'We can see who put the Frogjuice in my bag!'

'Let him be, George,' said Smithy.

George released Todd, who hopped back into Smithy's office. Fat George closed the door from the outside.

Smithy eyed Todd seriously. 'You are right,' he said. 'There is a camera in the locker room and we keep the films for seven days. I should have thought of it. Come with me.'

Todd followed Smithy out of his office and into a small room next door. In the room there were four security frogs. Against the far wall, stacked in neat rows, were hundreds of videocassette tapes, each marked with a number and a date. Smithy chose one of the tapes and handed it to a guard. 'Play this for me,' he said, 'on fast forward.'

The guard inserted the cassette into the slot of a video machine and pressed a button. On a screen, a black and white picture of the locker room came into view. Todd could clearly see his bag, hanging on a hook against the far wall.

'It looks like a still picture,' said the guard. 'Until somebody comes into the room that is.'

Every so often somebody did enter the locker room and each time the guard slowed the video. As long as the frog in the picture was not opening Todd's bag, the guard would speed the picture up again; this happened about a dozen times.

'Nearly at the end now,' said the guard.

'Are you sure you got the right video?' asked Todd, a trickle of sweat running slowly down his neck.

Smithy was about to answer when a flash of black moved across the screen. The guard slowed the video. A frog wearing a black suit had entered the locker room. Todd could not see who it was as they had their back to the camera. The frog hopped across to the far wall.

'Look!' shouted Todd pointing at the screen. 'In his hands!'

In the frog's hands were two bottles of Frogjuice and it was obvious to all watching the video what was going to happen next. The frog unclipped the top of Todd's bag and slipped the bottles inside. He secured the clip and turned towards the door and, of course, the camera. The frog was Sly Spawn.

'Well I never,' said Smithy, a look of astonishment on his face. 'What a miserable thing to do.'

Todd was not quite so surprised, but he was very upset and was shaking visibly.

'So what happens now?' he asked.

'Well, this is rather serious,' said Smithy. 'We must call the police right away; it is company policy. We always prosecute for theft.'

Todd just nodded. It did not feel at all nice getting another frog into trouble, but if this was the policy…

It only took Smithy a few minutes to make the call to the Frog City police station and when the call was over he looked at Todd.

'The police are having a busy day. There is an important sailing regatta at Lily Cove; most of the policefrogs are helping with the event. Two officers will be in my office tomorrow morning, at the start of the first shift. We will keep the video safe until then. Can you be here?'

Todd nodded.

'The police said, that as the Frogjuice did not actually leave the premises, there is no crime against the Frogjuice Corporation, but what Sly has done may constitute a crime against you personally. It is therefore up to you to press charges.'

'Not good,' thought Todd. That would really make an enemy of Sly.

'What if I don't press charges?'

Smithy thought for a moment.

Well, that is your choice,' he said. 'If you do press charges and Sly is found guilty then he will be sacked by the company.'

Smithy looked at Todd seriously.

'But if you do not press charges then the company cannot take any action against him, that's frog law I'm afraid, the company can only dismiss an employee for an issue with their timekeeping or their work, otherwise only for a proven criminal offence.'

It was with a heavy heart that Todd hopped home. He was pleased to be in the clear regarding the theft and Smithy said he was welcome back at work the following day. He did not, however, relish the thought of pressing charges against Sly.

He did not tell his mother about the day's events. She knew nothing about the Frogjuice incident and he did not want to worry her.

'How was the race today?' she asked when he hopped into the cottage.

'Oh it was a good one,' he lied. 'I did quite well.'

'That's good.'

After dinner, while his mother scrubbed the kitchen from top to bottom (for the second time that day), he sat in his room and pondered. Whether or not to press charges, that was the dilemma. He decided he would press charges. Why should Sly get away with the crime? He might do it to somebody else. He deserved it. But then he thought it was not such a good idea. It might make matters worse. What would Sly do next? Perhaps he should move on, forget about it. He wished the incident with the spiders had not happened. Perhaps it was his own fault for being involved in such a nasty trick.

There was a knock at the door, which was swiftly opened by his mother; as usual she thought it might be Todd's father. Following a brief exchange of words, his mother called him.

'Somebody to see you Todd, can you come down?'

Todd hopped down the stairs. A large toad, wearing black shorts, a white shirt and a black tie was squatting in the front room. In one hand he held a brown envelope.

'Hello,' said Todd warily.

Todd Tinpot?' enquired the toad. His voice was deep and gruff; Todd recognised the accent as coming from the poorer quarters of Toad Alley.

'That's me,' said Todd.

'My boss, Mr Victor Spawn, has instructed me to pay you a visit. He would like to…'

'You mean Sly's dad,' interrupted Todd.

The toad continued, 'Mr. Spawn is aware of the unfortunate

incident at the factory. He is also aware of your present, shall we say, "financial difficulties" and he would like to make you an offer.'

Todd's mother looked at Todd.

'What incident?' she asked. 'What is this toad talking about?'

Todd did not want to worry his mother but he did not appear to have much choice. Whilst the toad shuffled uncomfortably, he provided her with a brief account of what had occurred at the factory. When he had finished his mother looked shocked. They both looked at the toad.

'What kind of an offer?' Todd asked.

The toad looked embarrassed. 'In this envelope there is a bank cheque for two hundred gold coins. If you are of a mind to accept that the incident at the factory was, shall we say, a misunderstanding, then the money is yours.'

'You mean if I don't press charges.'

'That is exactly what Mr Spawn desires.'

Todd looked at his mother.

'Don't look at me,' she said. 'You should ask your father when he gets home.'

The toad looked confused.

'I thought your father was…'

'At work,' said Todd's mother firmly. 'He will be back in a little while.'

The toad looked very confused but he did not pursue the point. 'Mr Spawn would like an answer right away,' he said.

'But you will stay for a cup of wasp tea,' said Todd's mother, cheerfully.

The toad looked as if he might decline but Todd answered for him. 'I am sure he has time for one cup, while I think about Mr Spawn's offer.'

The toad nodded and Todd's mother disappeared into the kitchen.

If Todd had been confused earlier, he was even more confused now. Two hundred gold coins represented a fortune; it was enough to pay the rent for a whole lifetime and was double the amount a frog would receive for winning a Superfrog competition. It was not only himself he had to think about, but also his mother. What would happen to them if they lost the house? He looked at the envelope and the toad held it towards him.

'Take it,' said the toad. 'I would.'

'You're not me,' snapped Todd, surprised at the tone in his voice.

It was certainly a tempting offer. The envelope held the answer to all of their problems. He wondered what his father would do.

'It doesn't feel right,' he said to the toad, 'taking money so that a crime goes unpunished.'

'Then think of your mother,' said the toad. 'You owe it to her.'

Perhaps I do, thought Todd, but don't I also owe it to her to do what is right? What if I don't take it? What if I don't take it and I press charges against Sly?'

The toad looked Todd straight in the eye; it wasn't very nice to be on the receiving end of such a stare. 'That would not be a good idea. Mr Spawn likes his offers to be accepted.'

Todd's stomach churned when he realised this was probably some kind of threat. He imagined Victor Spawn with his expensive cigar, squatting in his expensive chair, in his expensive office, in his expensive building where he earned great wads of cash for himself and his spoilt son. Sly had called Todd a specky loser. Thinking about that made Todd very angry. It was not nice and now Todd was being threatened, and that was not nice either. He knew what he had to do.

'I think you should leave,' said Todd firmly. 'You can tell Mr Spawn that his money can buy many things, but it cannot buy me.'

The toad glared at him then turned and hopped towards the door.

As he opened it to leave, Todd spoke. 'What's all the fish food for?'

The toad turned around. Todd could see that he was shocked.

'Don't mess with things you don't understand,' said the toad seriously. He slammed the door; the cottage was quiet.

Todd's mother appeared with the tea. 'Has he gone?' she said, surprised.

'He's gone,' said Todd. 'I rejected his offer.'

'I'm sure you did the right thing,' she said pouring the tea. 'What was it he wanted again?'

'Nothing important,' said Todd. 'Nothing important.'

Todd was now certain Victor was up to no good. If there was a harmless explanation for the fish food then why had the toad looked so shocked when Todd had mentioned it?

That night he fell into the deepest sleep. In his dreams he was with his father and they raced together – through the woods, across the stream and along many paths and fields.

'You've changed,' said his father. 'You're not the frail little chap I used to know. You look stronger. You know how much I love you, don't you?'

Todd did know and even as he slept a smile spread across his face.

12. Slippery Goings On

Four days later Todd was at Toad Alley. He had missed the last two races and he was not feeling particularly fit. How had he ever convinced himself that there was the possibility of winning Superfrog? It was just a dream, a silly idea he should have dismissed from his mind long ago. In order to qualify for Superfrog, in sixteen days time, he would have to finish in a top three position in one of the next five races.

At the start arena one of Cleopatra's female friends, a competitor, was teasing Boris. 'Did you enjoy the last race Boris?' she said, winking at Cleopatra as she spoke. Rumour had it that Boris had got lost in the race at Ribbitt Shallows.

Boris took the bait. 'Pulled a muscle,' he said. 'Quite painful it was.'

'Don't give me pulled muscles,' said Cleopatra. 'I seem to remember you doing a full double back-flip for me after the race.'

Boris flipped a double backward somersault, landing perfectly on his flippers. 'Like that one?' he asked.

'Just like that one,' said Cleopatra.

Todd laughed. It was hard to feel glum with Boris around.

He was proud of himself for having done the right thing and not accepting the money from Victor Spawn. He had met with the police the morning after the visit from the toad and pressed charges. Sly had been suspended from work the same day and his court appearance would take place in a few days time.

'Five minutes before the start,' boomed a toad with a megaphone.

'We are going to stay together in today's race,' said Todd. 'After last night's rain there's a lot of water flowing and the stream looks rather nasty.'

'I went to look at it this morning after the gym,' said Boris. 'I've never seen it so big. There were some frogs kayaking.'

'From the kayaking centre upstream I expect,' said Cleopatra. 'It must have been instructors, maybe even the Frog Pond team.'

'Anyway, it was pretty scary,' said Todd. 'Too fast to swim across.'

'I expect everybody will use the log,' said Boris. 'That's the way Todd and I will go. You have to go upstream to get to it but I can't imagine anybody risking the jump. I tell you what, Cleo, why don't you watch the race from there?'

'I might just do that,' she said, 'although I might not be able to stay long enough to watch you back hoppers.'

'Ooooh!' said Boris, dropping to the ground, as if felled by an invisible arrow. 'I am mortally wounded and will never recover unless kissed by a princess in lemon coloured "Pike" trainers.'

Cleopatra ignored him and hopped away.

Todd looked at his watch. 'Come on, let's get to the start,' he said seriously.

'Chill out,' said Boris, still lying in the dirt. 'We've got ages yet.'

'Look this might not be important to you but I've go to…' Todd stopped himself in mid sentence.

'You've got to what?' asked Boris, in a not uncaring manner.

'Nothing,' said Todd. 'Let's just get to the start.' He hopped away with tears in his eyes, his glasses misting so that he could hardly see.

He and his mother had held each other tight that morning. It felt a bit weird and he was glad that his friends couldn't see him, but the pain was just too much to bear. The night before the Head Park Ranger had turned up at the cottage to deliver Todd's father's favourite spade.

'We found it close to the saplings he was planting,' said the ranger. 'Nothing else, just the spade.'

It was very distressing.

Before Boris caught up with him, Todd had dried his eyes and de-misted his glasses. They made their way to the start arena, outside of Toad Alley Town Hall. The competitors were in an excitable mood.

'I reckon I could jump it,' said one.

'No chance, you're one bug short of a swarm,' said another. 'Have you seen Viagra falls? If you don't make the jump then you're one dead frog.'

'What about going downstream and jumping the narrow gap?'

'Yellow Belly, Yellow Belly,' sang a number of frogs in unison.

'It's got to be the log.'

'I still reckon I might jump it.'

And so the chatter went on, until the toad with the gun stepped onto his pebble and fired his pistol.

Todd and Boris stuck close together for the first half of the race. 'Together until the log, then every frog for himself' was the agreement.

For the first time in any race Todd and Boris stayed close to the lead pack of six frogs right from the start. It was a risky strategy: work too hard in the first half of the race and be tired for the second half. Surprisingly, Sly was not racing, but Todd recognised his gang amongst the leaders, hopping along just slightly ahead of them. It was only as they neared the end of Sapper Straight that Todd and Boris began to drop behind. Boris appeared to be getting tired and Todd slowed his pace to stay with him.

'What's with you today?' asked Boris as they hopped along the straight. 'You're like a frog on a mission.'

I've got a cottage to save, thought Todd. 'Just feeling good today,' he answered. 'You drop back if you're struggling.'

'No way,' said Boris. 'Let's just slow a little and reserve some energy for after the log.'

Todd agreed and they hopped at a slightly slower pace.

'How's mother?' asked Boris.

'Not so good,' said Todd. 'Still feeding dad even though he's not there, and she holds conversations with him as well. It's almost as if he's in the room, but invisible.'

They worked their way methodically through Copse, picking their way carefully through the exposed roots that covered the ground. Sometimes it was faster to skirt wide around the base of a tree; at other times it was impossible to avoid climbing, crawling or hopping through the network of gnarly woodwork. At last they arrived at the stream where the two frogs rested for a moment.

'I'm glad that's out of the way,' gasped Todd, taking off his glasses and wiping them on his t-shirt. 'Dirt on the lenses; I could hardly see a thing those last dozen hops. 'Crikey!' he exclaimed after he had put his glasses back on his face. 'It looks even higher than it was this morning.'

The stream was running at full spate, almost in danger of bursting its banks. The dark water rushed down the channel, turning white as it poured over and around the many rocks and obstacles in its path. In some places there was more white water than dark water and every so often large sticks and branches were swept downstream, ending their journey wedged between rocks or stuck between gaps. Todd shuddered.

It took about twenty minutes for them to reach the log. The lead pack was already on the other side. Todd could see about ten or so spectators, including Cleopatra, standing on the far bank.

The log was about six inches wide and completely round. Every so often a branch protruded from its sides and, in two places, thick branch stumps extended vertically into the air.

'They are the tricky bits,' explained Boris. 'You have to go around them without slipping off. Hang onto them with your hands and swing your flippers around to the other side. I'll lead the way and you follow. Remember, don't look down.'

Boris jumped onto the log and slowly hopped along its length. Todd followed close behind, his heart beating rather faster than he would have liked. Beneath them the water roared.

About one third of the way across, Boris stopped. In front of him was the first of the two vertical branches. He gripped the branch with both hands and swung his flippers around it. For a fraction of a second, the only thing connecting Boris to the log was his grip on the branch. The frogs on the bank gasped. This was a good vantage point for spectators and the crowd had gasped in the same way for each competitor who had crossed.

'Your turn,' shouted Boris. 'Grip tight, don't look down and it's easy peasy.'

Todd felt his belly tighten. Two hops later he was in front of the branch. He looked down. The water below raced and swirled and for a second or two he felt mesmerized by its movement. He started to sway slightly.

'Don't look down!' shouted Boris. 'Look at me.'

Todd snapped back into reality and looked at Boris. Taking a deep breath he grasped the branch as tight as he possibly could and swung his flippers around to the other side. The small crowd gasped in unison. He was safely past the first branch and he breathed a huge sigh of relief.

After the first branch the second one seemed easier. The log itself was easily wide enough for hopping and, as long as he did not look down, swinging himself around the vertical branches was not so difficult. With both Boris and Todd safely past the second branch it was just a dozen or so hops to reach the far bank.

'You first,' said Boris. 'A little head start at the far end won't do you any harm.'

Cleopatra cheered from the crowd, forgetting for the moment that only a few moments ago she had noticed a toad hiding behind a stone a little further along the course; a toad in black shorts, a white shirt and a black neck tie. Sly's gang had crossed the log a few minutes earlier, huddling together for a short while, close to where Boris and Todd were now standing. She felt a little uneasy.

Todd was eager to get on with the race. It felt as if they had already spent a long time crossing the stream, and a number of competitors were close behind. He turned and hopped across the log, towards the bank.

What happened next was completely unexpected; to Todd it seemed as if his whole world changed into slow motion. In mid air, between his second and third hop, he noticed something on the log, something shiny and amber, something sticky – or something slippery.

'Not good,' he thought, a cold fear rushing through every vein in his body. In mid air, even in slow motion, there was little he could do.

The surface was indeed slippery and, when he landed, his flippers slid off the left side of the log. His face hit the log with a sickening thud, his glasses were knocked from his head and he fell toward the roaring white water below. The hard smack in the face dulled his senses, but he still knew what was happening and the fall to the water continued in slow motion. Everything changed when he hit the water. The slow motion world was replaced by a world of fury and speed, a cold, brown world that spun and trashed his body as if it were a useless piece of driftwood. Flashes of light appeared then disappeared with each spin. He knew what was happening yet he failed to resist. He watched as light filtered along a swirling strand of coiled air, marvelling at its beauty, before it disappeared into the darkness. He thought of his father and mother and of Boris, and Cleopatra. He was calm, without care and without fear. He was drowning.

Cleopatra screamed when Todd hit the water; the rest of the small crowd was, at first, too shocked to react. This was why the crowd was at the log; it was dangerous, exciting and a frog might fall. Now they had got their fall.

Boris did not have to think about following Todd into the water. He knew it was dangerous and he had weighed the risk within a fraction of a second. He dived into the swirling water only a second or two after Todd fell, entering the same dark, spinning world that would trash his body and assault his senses. But Boris was on full adrenaline and, unlike Todd, had not taken a knock to the head. When he saw the light he lunged for it, breaking the surface of the water and spinning his head wildly in his search for his friend.

Cleopatra and a number of other frogs hopped and leapt along the bank.

'Where is he?' screamed Boris, already drifting at speed downstream.

'We can't see him,' Cleopatra screamed back. 'He's downstream of you somewhere. We saw him to the left of that big rock but he disappeared under the water.'

Boris was heading fast towards the wrong side of the big rock. He swam as hard as he could across the current, only just managing to make the flume of water, which passed to its left. Once again he disappeared into the dark, spinning world and once again he aimed for the light and surged to the surface. Todd was nowhere to be seen. Boris was not a frog to panic, but this was not looking good, and he was running out of energy.

Under the water, Todd was unaware of the actions to save him; he was pretty much unaware of anything at all – drifting and dreaming, not breathing and not caring. His thigh bumped hard against a rock and he wondered why it didn't hurt. He hoped he hadn't damaged himself; he had races to win. He saw a flash of light. He felt the cold of the water on his body, and in his lungs. He had to do something. With one huge lunge, using the last remaining energy in his body, he broke through the surface of the water.

Cleopatra saw him first. 'Boris! I can see him, in the eddy behind the rock.'

But Boris was having problems of his own. He was a long way downstream and was being swept towards the falls.

Cleopatra kicked off her trainers and dived into the eddy where Todd was floating, face down in the water. It only took a few strides for her to reach him and put her arms around him. Swimming on her back, she kicked her way towards the bank, all the time making sure that Todd's head was out of the water. Once on the bank they were quickly surrounded by a group of spectators. With a great deal of luck one of the frogs was trained in First Aid and he took control, pumping Todd's chest and giving mouth to mouth resuscitation. It seemed to take forever but the young frog knew what he was doing.

'Come on, breathe,' he said, pumping Todd's chest for the umpteenth time.

Todd was certainly not his usual colour. 'A bit grey,' said Cleopatra later. He also had a very nasty gash, which ran from his left cheek to just above his right eye.

He spluttered and water gushed from his mouth. He coughed, took a breath and then spluttered again. This went on for a number of minutes, but gradually his colour returned and the coughing and spluttering decreased. Cleopatra sobbed gently; she could hardly bear to see her friend this way.

Boris, who had narrowly evaded the falls, pushed his way into the group that surrounded Todd. 'How is he?'

'He'll live,' said the first aid frog, 'but we need to get this gash on his head looked at.'

13. The Lizard

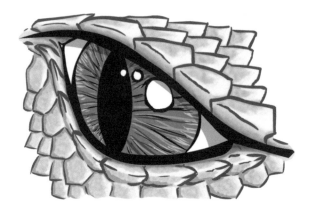

Todd was in Frog City hospital for two days. The gash on his face was not as serious as it had looked, but it had required four stitches. On the second day Boris paid a visit.

'I've brought you some bugs,' he said. 'Chocolate coated with mint dipped legs, and this month's edition of "Ribbitt!" magazine. There's a really cool advert for the new R5 Mosquito jet bike.'

'Thanks,' said Todd miserably. 'Where's Cleopatra?'

'She should be here anytime.'

'I'm coming out tonight. The Doctor says it's okay. It was the knock on the head which had them worried.'

'Did the police find any clues to what happened?' asked Boris.

'They only know that it was honey on the log. They talked to Sly's mates, but they all said they hadn't seen anything.'

'Do you think it was them?'

'Of course,' said Todd angrily. 'Everybody knows it was something to do with them; we just can't prove it.'

He was right. The police report stated "foul play in this incident is deemed highly likely" but there was no evidence to suggest who had put the honey on the log.

'The police came to see me this morning,' said Todd. 'But I can't remember a thing. I remember being on the log and then I woke up here, in hospital. Feels pretty weird.'

Todd left hospital that evening. Boris, who had obtained special permission to use his Frogjuice truck outside of working hours, drove him home.

'Fancy a few freebies off of the back?' laughed Boris as they pulled up outside of Todd's cottage.

'That is not such a good idea,' laughed Todd.

The two frogs stayed in the cab awhile, laughing and joking and talking about racing. They were in high spirits. Late that afternoon they had both received some good news. During the morning there had been a special meeting of the Frog Pond Racing Committee. Due to Todd's "accident" most of the meeting had been taken up with safety issues. A decision was made that the log would be out of bounds for all future races. It was not this that had made their spirits soar, but the announcement made at the end of the meeting. Todd and Boris were to be given special privileges to enter the Frog City Superfrog competition. In Boris's case, this was due to his outstanding bravery. In Todd's case, it was because, through no fault of his own, he was unable to compete in any of the three remaining qualification races (upon the orders of his doctor).

Todd slept fitfully that night. Cleopatra had told him of the toad hiding close to the log. He was sure that this was one of Victor's cronies, possibly even the toad that had visited the cottage. He also felt sure that Sly's mates had put the honey on the log.

He was also worried about his mother. She had fussed over him on his return from hospital, but she was still behaving in a very odd manner. When Boris had entered the cottage with Todd, she had called Boris "love" and had asked him whether he had had a good day at work. When Boris eventually left she had gone upstairs. Todd had found her sitting in the dark, clutching his dad's spade. He had taken the spade and tucked her up in her bed.

He also worried about the cottage. If he did not win Superfrog, or at least finish in second or third place, both he and his mother would very soon be homeless.

I have to win Superfrog, he thought, however impossible it seems. I have to do it.

The next morning he was up early. Against doctor's orders, he had to train: the Superfrog event was only twelve days away.

From the cottage he hopped to Toad Alley, the location for the Superfrog race. Very slowly, he completed the full length of the course: Spindler's Lane, Sapper Straight, Copse Wood, the stream (which was at normal flow and which he jumped without a problem), Meteor Rock and Sandy Beach. At the beach he sat himself down on a pebble, close to the edge of the pond. The sun warmed his back and the stitched gash on his face throbbed.

On the day of the Superfrog event, this vast expanse of pebbles, which separated the pond from the sand, would form a seating arena for over a thousand frogs and toads. From here the spectators would see the competitors as they entered the beach and they would cheer them on as they completed the final, gruelling, twenty-five metres of the race. Todd gazed out across the sand. The part of the race I'm not looking forward to, he thought. If I don't arrive here in the top three then it's all over.

The surface of the sand shimmered as he watched; it was going to be a very hot day. On the far side of the beach, a lizard crawled slowly and lazily towards the sand. 'Lizard racing,' thought Todd. 'Now that would be like watching paint dry.'

But then the lizard did a rather remarkable thing; it was something Todd had never seen a lizard do. It stood up high and straight, arched its back, and sprinted across the sand in Todd's direction. It did not crawl, as one would expect, or hop, like a frog; it used only its hind legs. One after the other they swung outwards, then forwards, until they were moving so fast that they became a blur. Leaving a cloud of dust and sand in its wake the lizard crossed the sand in hardly any time at all. When it reached the pebbles, it flopped back onto all fours, scurried across them, stuck its long pink tongue into the water, and drank.

Todd was astonished. Never in his wildest dreams had he imagined that a lizard could move so fast. He hopped across the sand to where the lizard was taking refreshment.

'Hey. Mr. Lizard. Can you spare a moment of your time?'

The lizard surveyed Todd with a large beady eye, continuing to drink as he did so. 'The name's Gecko,' said the lizard, when he had finished drinking. 'Gecko Plink.'

Todd,' said Todd. 'Todd Tinpot.'

'I know. You're the frog who fell from the log. I read about it in the newspaper.'

'I saw you speeding across the beach,' said Todd. 'Why did you do that?'

Gecko looked out across the sand. 'There was a snake, in that bush over there. I feel he wanted me for a snack and a snack I did not fancy to be.'

'Could you teach me to cross the sand like that?'

'And why might I want to do that? In this weather all I desire is to sleep.'

Todd told Gecko everything: about his father's disappearance, his mother's strange behaviour, the problems with Sly and the offer from Victor. While he spoke, Gecko sprawled out on a large flat pebble. When Todd had finished he wondered if Gecko had indeed drifted off to sleep.

But Gecko was not asleep. 'Meet me here this evening,' he said, 'and each evening between now and your race. Now leave me alone as I am very sleepy.'

Todd thanked him profusely; Gecko was asleep before he had spoken his fourth word.

During the twelve days between meeting Gecko and the day of the big race, Todd trained like he had never trained before. Not at the gym, as he had done previously, but on the Toad Alley course. In the mornings he concentrated on the first half of the course, between the start and the stream. In the afternoons he concentrated on the second half of the course, between the stream and Sandy Beach. Each evening he met with Gecko. They did not train at the beach; Gecko had suggested they train in secret and he took Todd to a similar stretch of sand some distance away.

The days seemed to fly by. Todd's head healed quickly and ceased to throb or sting. Sly had his day in court, receiving a small fine and a community service order (it was rumoured that he had got off lightly following intervention from his father). Todd's mother was still behaving in a strange manner but at least she did not appear to be getting any worse. Most days Todd would meet Boris and Cleopatra, either at the Green Cafe, for bugs or somewhere else for cocktails or ice cream. Boris was unaware how hard Todd was training; he was training hard himself, mainly at the gym. Cleopatra had found out. She was very fond of Todd and knew him well enough to know that he was keeping something from her. She had questioned him so hard that he had felt he had no choice. He had told her everything, including about the cottage and his desire to win Superfrog.

'You're very brave,' she said, kissing him on the cheek. 'But it's a very big race and the best in the world will all be there.'

Todd had known she was preparing him for possible disappointment.

'I know,' he said. 'I also know that there is little chance of me even finishing in the top twenty.'

But he had lied. He had to believe that he could do it. What other option was open to him?

'Only when you know you can win will it be possible,' Gecko had said. 'When you close your eyes, you should see yourself winning. If you cannot, then you will not be able to win.'

At Toad Alley, and with just two days to go before the race, preparations were well underway. This was a much more important event than the local races and large crowds were expected. Posts and ropes formed a fence on both sides of the racing route. At key points large stands, raised areas of seating for twenty, thirty or even fifty spectators, were being constructed. Spectators would have to pay of course and tickets for these seats were very expensive.

For the first time in frog racing history the event was to be broadcast live on Frog TV and cameras were being placed all along the course. Because of Todd's accident, the Log was not going to be an option in the race and frogs would jump the stream above Viagra Falls. The stream would not be running high for this event, whatever the weather the night before. Two days previously, five beavers had started work on a huge dam and it was already half complete. On the day of the race the stream would run almost dry. The organisers were taking no chances; a frog being swept over the falls would not be good publicity.

14. Victor's Mansion

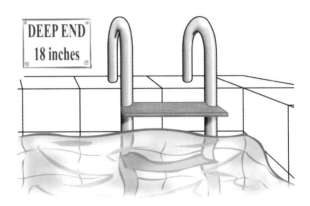

With two days to go before the race Todd, Boris and Cleopatra met at the Green Cafe for an early breakfast. Due to them being competitors, Todd and Boris had been given three days off work: two days for last minute training and one day for the race.

'Boris,' whispered Todd while Cleopatra was ordering from the sales counter. 'How do you fancy a little adventure?'

'What sort of adventure?' whispered Boris, 'and why are we whispering?'

'I want to go to Victor's mansion again, to find out what's happening there. I can't get it out of my head that it has something to do with my dad's disappearance.'

'Sounds fun to me, but we saw everything from the tower. I can't think what else we can do.'

'We could climb over the wall and take a look around,' said Todd, glancing in the direction of Cleopatra who was still in the queue for drinks. 'We could go tonight, just after it gets dark.'

'You're mad, and I bet you Cleo will agree.'

'We shouldn't tell Cleo, it might be dangerous and I don't want her involved.'

'Great!' said Boris indignantly. 'It's okay for me to get roughed up by one of Victor's henchman, or swallowed whole by some guard-snake.'

'There aren't any snakes Boris, that's just a rumour. I'll go on my own then.'

'No way. I'm not missing out on all the fun.'

The matter was settled. That evening they would climb the wall into Victor's mansion and take a look around. They would tell Cleopatra they were going to the cinema to watch Goldflipper – the latest James Pond film. They knew that Cleo wouldn't be able to go; she would be frogsitting her little nephew.

'What are you two talking about?' asked Cleopatra when she returned with the drinks.

'Oh, just planning our strategy for the race,' said Boris. But of course he was not telling the truth and Cleopatra was left unaware of their plans.

That evening the two frogs met outside of Todd's cottage. As agreed, both were dressed in black and Todd had a large torch and a long rope.

'I feel like a right criminal,' said Boris. 'All I need is a bag with "swag" written on it.'

Todd laughed. 'Come on, let's go.'

An hour later they were standing underneath the wall that surrounded the mansion. It was certainly high and a series of sharp metal spikes ran along its top. It was obviously designed to stop anybody getting in, or, as Boris was wondering, to stop something getting out.

There was no moon and, with the exception of the mansion, everywhere was in darkness. The wind whistled eerily through the trees and an owl hooted in the distance.

'I'm not sure this is such a good idea,' whispered Boris. 'How about we go to the pictures after all?'

'No way,' said Todd. 'You go if you want but I've got to do this.'

Todd took one end of the neatly coiled length of rope and made a loop at one end; he secured the loop with a knot. Grasping the coil in one hand and the loop in the other, he looked up to the top of the wall.

'I've just got to get the loop over one of those spikes and we've got our way in,' said Todd.

It took at least a dozen attempts before the loop finally located one of the spikes. Todd pulled hard on the rope and pronounced it secure.

'Okay, he said. 'I'll go first and you follow. When we're both at the top we'll pull the rope up and then use it to climb down the other side.'

In the bushes behind them a twig cracked loudly; the two frogs jumped. Boris shone the torch in the direction of the noise.

'Who's there,' he hissed.

The bush swayed slightly in the breeze. To their left a rabbit darted into its burrow.

'Come on Boris, it'll just be an animal or something, you're just a bit jittery.'

Todd climbed the rope and pulled himself onto the top of the wall. From here he could see the rear of the mansion, its garden and pool lit by a variety of strategically placed security lights. Although very large, the mansion was not a fancy building. It was built of stone, it was three storeys high and almost perfectly square.

'Any snakes in the grounds,' said Boris climbing up next to Todd. 'If we see one then…'

'Shhh…' said Todd. 'I can see somebody.'

A large toad, dressed in black shorts, tie and jacket, and a white shirt, hopped out of a door at the rear of the house. Todd and Boris flattened themselves against the top of the wall. The toad hopped from the mansion to the pool then made his way around the pool and back through the door from where he had emerged.

'That's the toad who came to the cottage,' whispered Todd.

He pulled the dangling rope up onto the top of the wall then dropped it into the grounds of the mansion. Before he had a chance to ask himself if this was such a good idea he grasped the rope, swung his legs over the edge of the wall and slid down, landing firmly on the grass below. He looked up towards Boris.

'Boris,' he hissed. 'Boris, come on down.'

Boris's frightened eyes appeared over the edge of the top of the wall. 'Just give it a few minutes,' he whispered. 'I want to see if a snake gets you.'

'Thanks a lot,' hissed Todd. 'Look, there's nothing down here and anyway it's illegal to have guardsnakes unless you work for the government.' Todd had made this up but he really didn't want to do this alone.

Boris slid down the rope and landed with a thump next to Todd. 'Ouch.'

'Okay,' said Todd. 'Let's hop across the grass and hide in the shadows. See those trees at the bottom of the garden, we'll head for those.'

Hopping close to the wall and staying in the shadows the two frogs made their way slowly towards the trees. Todd didn't have a clue what it was he was looking for and Boris just wished that they were at the pictures.

Todd stopped under a bush and motioned Boris to do the same.

Ahead of them, and previously hidden from view behind a group of plants, was a small rectangular concrete building; its windows were secured with bars. On the side of the building was a metal door, secured with a large padlock.

'Do you think that's where they keep the snakes?' whispered Boris.

'Shut up about snakes. We'll check it out on the way back.'

In the distance a door could be heard opening. Todd and Boris hopped into a dark area behind an old tree stump.

'It's the toad again, he's heading our way,' said Boris, a bead of perspiration rolling down his cheek.

'Don't panic Boris, we're dressed all in black and he won't be able to see us. He's probably going to do the same circuit as he did before.'

And that's almost exactly what he did do, but instead of hopping around the pool and returning to the door, he disappeared down some steps on one side of the pool. 'Hey,' said Boris, 'he's gone underground!'

'Weird,' said Todd. 'Let's see if he comes back up again. If he clears off we'll go check it out. I think he's on some kind of regular patrol.'

The two frogs did not have long to wait. The toad, as Todd had predicted, soon appeared. He hopped his way around the pool and disappeared back into the door at the rear of the mansion.

'Let's go,' said Todd. 'Follow me.'

The two frogs hopped across the grass towards the pool. At the top of the steps, Todd waited for Boris to catch up.

'We've got to be quick. I reckon we've got about ten minutes before the toad comes back.' He proceeded down the steps and Boris hopped cautiously after him.

The steps were steep and at the bottom was a door. Todd pushed and it opened easily. The two nervous frogs hopped inside. They were now underneath the level of the ground outside and it was pitch black. Todd switched on his torch.

'It's just a corridor,' said Boris. 'Look, no more doors. Nothing interesting. Let's go.'

'Just hang on a minute. What's the point of having a corridor that goes nowhere?'

Todd moved the beam of his torch around the corridor. The floor, ceiling and left wall were made simply of concrete but the wall to the right was not the same at all.'

'It's glass,' laughed Todd. 'Look, you can see into the pool.' He angled the beam of the torch at the glass and moved it slowly around. 'Look, you can see the beam shining through the pool; see those bubbles and I can see…'

Todd did not finish his sentence. In just a fraction of a second each and every one of his senses shut down. He wanted to cry out, or fall backwards or hop. But for a second or two he just froze. Staring back at him from inside the pool and lit by the beam of the torch was something terrible, with more teeth in one mouth than Todd could ever have imagined. He was chilled to his very core. He knew what it was – he had seen the film – it was a huge Pike.

Boris also saw what was in the pool, but for some reason – perhaps because he was not quite so close – he did not freeze. Moving faster than he had ever moved before, he hopped up the stairs, across the grass and hid, quivering with fright, in the darkness behind the tree stump.

Todd was only a few seconds behind him, but he wasn't thinking straight at all and at the top of the stairs he went in a different direction, towards the lights of the house, straight into the path of the toad.

'Well, well, well,' said the toad grabbing Todd roughly by his shirt. 'Look what I've found. Young Mr. Tinpot snooping around. Now Mr Spawn is not going to be too pleased about this.'

'But there's… something… inside the pool,' said a very wide-eyed Todd, still shocked by what he had just seen.

'Now that is even more serious,' said the toad. 'Victor is not going to be happy at all.'

Todd was pushed roughly through the door at the rear of the mansion and even more roughly through a second door into a large room, the walls of which were adorned with large oil paintings. Each of the paintings showed a member of the Spawn family – past and present. A huge rat-skin rug covered the varnished wooden floor and at one end of the rug were the only pieces of furniture in the room: a large oak chair and desk. Squatting on the chair, dressed in a black pin stripe suit and smoking a huge cigar, was a large frog: it was Victor Spawn.

The toad pushed Todd in front of the desk. 'I found him snooping around the grounds. It's the Tinpot kid and he's seen what's in the pool.'

Victor stared at Todd from behind the desk. 'Well, well,' he said. 'Your family do seem to be poking their noses where they do not belong.'

'Why did you say family?' asked Todd angrily. 'What do you know about my dad?'

'Your dad's here alright,' replied Victor. 'You'll get to meet him very soon. He was a snooper as well. Like father, like son, I guess. We caught him spying on us from the watchtower and, how shall I put it, we have him here as our guest.'

'If you have hurt him I…'

'You will what?' said Victor calmly. 'I don't think that you are in any position to threaten me. Like your father you will remain here as my guest until my plan goes into operation.'

'What plan?' asked Todd.

'The plan that will ensure Frog Pond's reputation as a tourist resort is damaged beyond repair; the plan that will see all the tourists flocking to Las Mega. In a few days time the Pike that you saw in the pond will be fully-grown. Nine of them, bred by myself, will be released into Frog Pond. All I have to do is a pull a lever. The pool is connected by an underground tunnel and this leads directly to the pond. I got the idea from the Pike film.'

'That's evil,' said Todd angrily. 'Frogs and toads might be killed before the order is given to keep everybody clear of the water. If they can't go into the water the tourists won't want to visit Frog pond; all of the tourist businesses will fail.'

'And Las Mega will thrive,' said Victor, sucking hard on the big cigar. 'Lock him up.'

The toad grabbed Todd roughly and dragged him, struggling, from the room – through the two doors, across the grounds and past the pool – to the small building with the barred windows he had seen earlier. The toad unlocked the door, pushed Todd inside and locked it again.

He returned to find Victor in a very bad mood.

'I don't like this at all. Maybe he isn't alone. Let the snakes out.'

'Right away.'

Back at the tree stump Boris was considering what to do. Things were not looking good. He had seen Todd being locked up. Should he try to rescue him? Should he climb back over the wall and raise the alarm? He decided on the latter. He hopped from the tree stump to the wall. He would stick close to its base, use the shadows for cover and climb the wall using the rope.

'Psssst!'

Boris stopped hopping and shrunk back into the shadows.

'Boris, up here, on the wall.'

Boris looked up. Sitting on top of the wall was Cleopatra.

'What are you doing here?' he asked, surprised.

'The babysitting was cancelled. I went to Todd's house and saw you two acting weird in black, so I followed you. That was me you heard in the bushes.'

'Todd's been locked up and…'

'I know,' said Cleopatra. 'I saw it from the top of the wall. I called my mum on the mobile and she's called the police. They should be here soon.'

'Tell them not to go in the pool,' whispered Boris.

'What?'

'It doesn't matter. I'll tell you later. I need to get out of this place.'

Boris started to hop towards the rope.

'Boris,' hissed Cleopatra.

'What now?'

'Near the pool, look!'

Boris stopped hopping and looked to his left. Sliding slowly across the grass was a snake; it was staring directly at him. 'Oh dear,' was all he managed to say and his heart thudded hard in his chest.

It was a good ten hops to the rope; there was no way he would arrive there before the snake got to him. Instinctively he grabbed a small branch from the ground. He would have to stand and fight. The snake slid closer and closer until it was only a few inches away. For the second time that day, Boris found himself looking into the eyes of something that wanted to eat him. He raised the branch. The snake raised itself as if ready to strike. Its eyes glazed over, it showed its fangs and then… its head exploded.

'Cool,' said Boris. 'I've never seen that before.'

'Boris,' shouted Cleopatra. 'The police, they're here. One of them got the snake with a catapult, what a shot!'

Cleopatra was right. A dozen or more ropes had appeared over the wall and uniformed policefrogs, all carrying high-powered catapults, were climbing down into the grounds. Some were already in the grounds and Boris could see three entering the house by the rear door. Close to the pool another snake dropped to the ground, felled by a pebble from a catapult. The police were taking no chances; this operation had taken many days of planning – the call about Todd being kidnapped had just brought things forward a few days.

'Excellent,' exclaimed Boris. 'Just in the nick of time.'

Inside the small building, Todd was unaware of what was happening outside. When the toad had locked the door it had taken a few moments for his eyes to become used to the dim interior. When his father spoke, Todd had jumped almost clean out of his skin.

'Todd, is that you?'

Todd and his father held each other tight for very many minutes; the tears flowed freely. When they had recovered from the shock of seeing one another, Todd's father told him what had happened: how he had spied on the mansion from the watchtower, how he had seen Victor and Sly putting the small Pike into the pool and how Victor's toad guards had kidnapped him. He had been in this small building ever since.

'What are they going to do with us?' Todd asked.

'I overheard one of the toads talking,' his father replied. 'Apparently Victor didn't know what to do with me. I thought that I was going to be Pike food. Now, apparently, he plans to hypnotise me and I suppose he intends to do the same to you. The toad said there is a frog who can do that sort of thing – make you forget things. I think he's coming in a few days.'

Todd had just started telling his father about his mother's depression when they heard the lock on the door being opened; the door swung ajar.

'Crikey,' said Todd. 'It's the police.'

An hour later and Todd, Boris, Cleopatra and Todd's father were at Frog City police station. They remained there until very late. Todd had worried whether they might be in trouble, but it was quite the opposite and the police were delighted with the outcome. Apparently, the raid on the mansion had not been due to take place for another four days. From what the police knew now that would have been too late, and the Pike would have already been released into the pond. Up until today, the police had not been aware of the Pike in the pool. They had been planning to raid the mansion for another reason altogether: tax evasion.

When Todd and his father eventually arrived home it was very late and the house was quiet. Todd's father hugged him before hopping quietly into the room where Todd's mother was sleeping. The noise and ribbitting that erupted a few moments later, were enough to bring a tear to the eye of any young frog and Todd sat on his bed and cried with happiness.

15. One Day To Go

It was the day before the big race. Frog City was buzzing with the news about the raid on Victor's mansion. Many frogs had recently watched "Pike" at the cinema and the newspapers took up the story with vigour. Typical was the headline in the Frog Pond Times "PIKE HORROR – FROG POND SAVED" or The Daily Reed "LAS MEGA BOSS IN PIKE TERROR" (with a drawing of a huge Pike's face staring out at its readers). The newspapers were particularly eager to state how close Frog Pond and its tourist industry had been to a major catastrophe.

Apparently, when the police entered the mansion, Victor had already flicked the switch, which opened the gates leading from the pool to the underground tunnel, and fed into the pond. The police had to grapple him to the ground and flick the switch from the "open" to the "closed" position. It was a close call: if the gate had opened another few inches then the smallest of the six Pike might have been able to swim free.

Victor, Sly and all of the toads employed at the mansion had been arrested and the papers hinted that a trial would take place in a few weeks time. Nobody was quite sure what would happen to the Pike, but the rumour was the Frog City Aquarium would look after them.

At Todd's house everybody was happy, especially Todd's mother. She wouldn't be parted from his father for even a second. Todd had never seen her so happy.

When his father found out that Todd was to compete in Superfrog he was amazed, and extremely proud. 'Your mother and I will be there,' he said. 'Cheering you on.'

Todd's father hoped that he would be able to get his old job back; the frog who was doing it at the moment was only temporary. Whether they could save the cottage or not was another matter; they were in a lot of debt and the council was not known for bending the rules.

That evening Boris and Todd travelled to Toad Alley on flipper. Boris's father had agreed that they could stay on site in the family's small caravan and he had towed it to the camping area that morning. Cleopatra would meet them early the next day. The two frogs were highly excited.

'Look at all the tents,' said Todd. 'There must be a thousand or more.'

All over the field frogs were putting up tents, lighting barbecues, chatting or training.

'The caravans must be in the next field,' said Boris, 'on the other side of the trees.'

They found the caravan without trouble and put their rucksacks inside. There was a chill in the air and they both put on their fleece jackets.

'Barbecue time,' said Boris. He flipped a full backward somersault. 'Bags me light it.'

Whilst Boris set up and lit the barbecue, Todd knocked up a bench from two flat pebbles and a piece of branch. He located the Frogjuice that they had purchased earlier and poured each of them a drink.

'To winning Superfrog,' he said, tapping his glass against Boris's.

'And to families,' said Boris, and they raised their glasses to their mouths and drank.

Boris did a good job of the barbecue and the two frogs were soon tucking into a hearty meal of boiled rice and, it has to be said, rather burnt King Cockroach.

As darkness fell, many more frogs arrived and the atmosphere in the camping fields became increasingly charged. Many frogs had purchased hand-operated air horns. Every so often one of the horns would sound, resulting in a reply from hundreds of other horns.

'It's like the biggest party in the world,' said Boris. 'I've never seen anything like it.'

Across the two fields, frogs ate, drank and made merry, and the smoke from a thousand or more barbecues filled the air with an assortment of intoxicating smells. Almost every tent or caravan had at least one small light. Spread out across the fields they resembled a mass gathering of top-grade glow-worms.

Todd and Boris cheered as the first of many fireworks screeched into the night, exploding against the dark sky and cascading magnificently back towards the earth.

It was rather late when they retired to their beds. The merry making, horns and fireworks continued late into the night, well after the two frogs had fallen fast asleep.

16. The Superfrog Championships

Todd and Boris were awakened shortly after dawn by a loud and persistent knocking on the caravan door – it was Cleopatra.

'Wow,' said Boris rubbing the sleep from his eyes. 'Look at you!'

She had certainly dressed for the occasion: new Oaklite sunglasses, a light pink and very short Chuggi skirt, and a white t-shirt, which left her green midriff completely exposed. Across the front of the t-shirt, in block capitals, was the word "HOP" (HOP is a famous Frog City boutique). To complete the outfit she wore a straw hat with a pink bow.

'I'll take you to dinner,' said Boris, 'straight after I win Superfrog.'

'Toads might fly,' laughed Cleopatra. 'And anyway, you won't win anything without a breakfast inside of you. I just happen to have brought you something.'

The three frogs chattered excitedly as they ate the bluebottle sandwiches that Cleopatra had provided. There was one bottle of Frogjuice left over from the previous evening and they shared it between them.

'There are thousands of frogs out there,' said Cleopatra. 'I've never seen anything like it.'

'It said in the paper that there's a team from the Amazon,' said Boris. 'Completely red they are – like berries.'

Todd laughed, he had seen pictures of red frogs but had never seen one for real. Although he hid it well, he was feeling extremely nervous, his stomach churned and bumped as if something in there was alive.

'Let's go take a look around,' he said.

There were a good two hours until the start of the race and the three frogs hopped their way slowly towards the start arena: the large flat plaza in front of Toad Alley Town Hall. As Cleopatra had said, it was very busy and many thousands of spectators filed along the paths into the town.

'Look! There's Tessa,' shouted Boris as they approached the plaza, 'under the trees, being interviewed by Frog TV. She's the fastest female racer in the world and she's pretty gorgeous as well.'

Cleopatra jumped onto Boris's shoulders for a better look and Boris beamed with pleasure.

'Cor!' said Cleopatra. 'There's Foxy as well. Look at those thighs. I've got a picture of him on my bedroom wall.'

Todd's heart sank. Foxy had won the last Superfrog event at Atlantis; he was very fast. Under the trees he could see some of the other superstars: Matty from the UK, Cheung from China, Zimmer from Germany and Renco from Holland, the world's fastest frogs, all waiting to be interviewed by Frog TV. What was I thinking of, thought Todd. Why did I ever believe I had a chance against these guys? He felt very miserable.

'They're not gods, just frogs like you,' said a voice from behind him.

Todd turned around. 'Gecko! I didn't know you were coming!'

'I thought I should support my favourite racing frog.'

Todd introduced Gecko to Boris and Cleopatra. 'My personal coach, he's been giving me a few tips.'

Gecko, who had been standing upright the whole time, smiled and puffed out his chest.

'You are a mysterious one,' said Boris. 'Your own personal coach, eh?'

Todd laughed. Gecko's arrival had cheered him up. I can win, he thought. They are just frogs like me and I bet they're nervous as well.

'Todd Tinpot?'

Todd turned around. Standing in front of him were three frogs. One of the frogs held a microphone and another carried a large camera on his shoulder. Todd recognised the third frog as Phillipe, a French frog and ex-Superfrog winner, who now worked for Frog TV Sports.

'A few words for Frog TV?' said the frog with the microphone.

'But… but,' stammered Todd, but the cameras were already rolling.

'Live broadcast number 5198, rolling, three, two, one and… action!'

'Well folks, we've spoken to the cream of the frog racing world and it looks like we are in for one heck of a race. But what is going through the mind of some of the other competitors here at Toad Alley? Todd Tinpot is one of these competitors. Todd, are you looking forward to the race?'

A very large microphone appeared in front of Todd's face.

'Er… I think so, a little nervous but…'

Before he could continue, the commentator pulled the microphone away. 'He's a little nervous and we don't blame him for that do we. Phillipe?'

'Certain, I do say non,' said Phillipe. 'Zee day zat I win Superfrog I was, how you say, scared stiffy.'

'Ha, ha, ha. He's a card, isn't he folks? Never tires of reminding us of when he won Superfrog. Ha, ha, ha. I do love the French. I can just imagine our Phillipe as a little boy, eez little onions on eez little andlebarz on eez little bicyclette.'

Cleopatra was behind Todd, hovering in the background so that she might be seen on television.

'But we are not in France today folks. If you have only just joined us we are live at Frog City for the Superfrog Championships and we are talking to competitor number 87, Todd Tinpot. Viewers at home might recognise this brave young competitor. Not so long ago he was almost killed, right here at Toad Alley. How's the scar healing Todd?'

'Er... it's coming on fine thanks and I'm ready to race.'

'A brave competitor indeed folks, which is just the sort of spirit we've come to expect at Superfrog. Join Phillipe and myself in a short while for the start of the race; break a flipper!'

Todd looked surprised and Boris laughed. 'Don't worry,' he said. 'That's his catchphrase.'

'I'm his agent,' said Gecko sidling up to Todd and peering into the camera.

'Cut!' shouted the commentator. 'Sorry lizard, time for the adverts.'

'Fifteen minutes to the start,' boomed a loud voice from the speakers dotted around the plaza. All spectators should leave the plaza.'

'This is it,' said Boris.

'Good luck to the both of you,' said Cleopatra, hugging Boris and Todd in turn. 'See you at the finish.'

'Good luck,' said Gecko, winking at Todd.

Within a few minutes, the only frogs in the plaza were the competitors: one hundred and fifty-five of the fittest and fastest frogs of the day. Every frog was wearing a bright green numbered bib. Todd was number 87, Boris number 88. The Frogjuice Corporation sponsored the bibs and the word "Frogjuice" ran across the top of each and every one.

'Best of luck old chap,' said Boris, as the final three-minute countdown commenced.

'Same to you big guy,' said Todd.

He turned and faced the start line. He breathed slowly and deeply, just as Gecko had taught him.

'Think of the inward breath as power entering your body,' Gecko had said. 'Every breath in is power, every breath out is a negative thought leaving the body.'

Todd focused only on his breathing and slowly the sights and sounds around him faded; they were no longer important. I can do it, he thought, I believe that I can do it.

The starting pistol fired. The crowd cheered. The race was on.

Todd found the hop along the High Street quite difficult. With over a hundred and fifty frogs in the race, it was very crowded. Competitors jostled for position as they hopped and more than once, he was elbowed in the side. The situation improved as the mass turned right onto Spindler's lane. He was about a third of the way from the front, exactly where he wanted to be.

The houses that ran along both sides of the lane were three or four stories high. Every door, window and balcony was filled with spectators who cheered and ribbitted as the race passed by. Seen from above, from the Frog TV helicopter, the competitors resembled a giant green snake, weaving its way through the town towards Sapper Straight.

I can do it, thought Todd. I can do it.

Sapper Straight was where he had planned to make his way into the lead pack. He felt strong and increased his speed, moving quickly past a number of other competitors. He knew he was pushing his luck; he was using a lot of energy, which might be required later in the race. But this was a part of his plan, a plan that had taken him ten days to devise. He wasn't going to wimp out now.

By the end of Sapper Straight, he was close to the rear of the lead pack, thirty or so of the fastest frogs in the race. The pack entered Copse and the crowd in the Copse seating arena roared with excitement.

'When you get to Copse,' Gecko had said. 'Forget about every frog in the race except those ahead of you. Now you are in a new race.'

At the time, Todd did not understand. He did now.

'Thirty frogs,' he thought to himself, 'this is a thirty-frog race.' The thought of there only being thirty frogs in the race spurred him on and he hopped through Copse at a good pace. He did not take quite the same route as the other competitors. It wasn't much different: left of a tree where they went right, right of a root where they went left, under a branch that they chose to hop; it was that sort of thing. During the last few days, using a stopwatch, he had worked out the most efficient route. As he emerged from Copse, he noticed one of the huge Frog TV plasma screens; he was in twenty-second place.

Again he remembered what Gecko had said. 'When you get to the stream, forget about everybody behind you. Look only at the frogs ahead. That is your new race. Whatever happens now, do not allow a single frog to overtake you.'

This new race had only twenty-two entries; a wave of excitement surged through Todd's body.

One by one the lead pack jumped the stream (running at a trickle due to the beaver's dam). The frog ahead of Todd did not quite make it, slipping on the far bank and rolling into the muddy water below.

Twenty-first, thought Todd greedily, as he cleared the stream, surprised at his own lack of feeling.

Meteor Rock loomed up ahead of the lead competitors and they hopped towards it. They were beginning to tire. The rock was covered in spectators; these were the most expensive seats for the race. On top of the rock, a Frog TV camera zoomed in on the lead pack.

The leading ten competitors passed to the right side of the rock and the crowd cheered and ribbitted them on.

'Foxy, Foxy, Foxy,' was the chant from one group.

'Come on Tessa,' cried another.

It was Foxy who was in the lead at this point, closely followed by Renco, Tessa and an unknown Greek frog called Zeus.

Todd approached the rock and the frogs in front of him followed the leaders to the right. This is it, thought Todd, they'll think I'm bonkers but here goes. He did not follow the other frogs to the right of the rock, instead he turned left; he took the longer route.

'What's he doing?' shouted one of the spectators.

'He's gone mad,' shouted another.

The camera on the rock swung around and focused on Todd, who was already disappearing, out of sight, around the back of the rock.

'Something extraordinary,' shouted the commentator. 'Todd Tinpot, competitor number 87, has taken a different route! Phillipe, why do you suppose he has done such a thing?'

'I am devoid of zee reasoning,' said Phillipe. 'It eez certainly zee way longest; it eez much zee taller way.'

The camera swung back to the main race, where Renco was hard on the flippers of Foxy.

But Todd did know what he was doing. Again and again he had timed the two routes around the rock and each time the longer route was faster, a good three minutes faster. Although the distance was greater, the ground was firm. On the right side it was marshy and this made it extremely hard going, and very tiring.

Renco overtook Foxy shortly before they passed the furthest tip of the rock. Tessa was now in third place and Zeus was doing very well in fourth. As they passed the end of the rock the crowed roared and the air horns blared, but not because of anything to with Foxy, or Renco. They were cheering Todd who had appeared from the left side of the rock and slipped into fifth place. The camera on the rock zoomed in on Todd, and in homes around the world frogs and toads went wild.

Todd was tired now; his thighs ached as they had never ached before and he wondered if he had overdone it. Ahead of him there was Sandy Beach – and Renco, Foxy, Tessa and Cheung. For some unknown reason Todd's concentration lapsed. He thought of those who had bullied him at school, and he thought of Sly.

Who did you think you were, calling me a specky loser, he thought. I'm going to show *you*. I'm going to show everybody.

All of the top five frogs started their hop across the beach. At the finish the crowd was already cheering, using their air horns to spur their heroes on. Renco was still in the lead and Foxy was close behind. The frogs were hopping as fast as their tired muscles would permit.

At the edge of the sand Todd stopped. He took a deep breath and, remembering what Gecko had taught him, he set out across the sand.

'Imagine the sand is hot,' Gecko had said, 'as hot as the red of the fire. Skim the sand with your flippers, as light and as fast as you can. Hopping in sand is slow; you land hard and your flippers sink. Running is faster. Keep your back straight, your head high and run. Whatever you do, you must resist the instinct to hop.'

Todd moved across the sand at twice the speed of any of the other frogs, his legs swinging outwards and forwards one after the other, skimming the sand so lightly that it was hardly even marked.

'Left… right… left… right… left… right,' he gasped as each of his flippers landed. All of the training was paying off. When he had first tried to run it had seemed impossible, the natural urge to hop overriding all of his attempts. Time after time he had failed and time after time Gecko had urged him on.

'You can do it,' Gecko had said. 'The more you practise the easier it will become.'

And it did become easier. Day after day Todd had trained with Gecko and each day he had perfected his technique. On their last training session together he had managed thirty steps, without reverting to the hop, and Gecko had cheered him every step of the way.

'You are ready,' Gecko had said after that last session, and for the first time in his life, Todd had embraced a lizard.

But today was not just training. This was the real thing and Todd was giving it everything, running across the sand as if his life depended upon it. He passed Cheung in a moment, the cloud of sand and dust in his wake causing the Chinese frog to disappear completely from view.

The crowd could hardly believe what they were seeing. Never before had a frog done anything other than hop. Hopping was what frogs did. When Todd passed Zeus and then Tessa, they went completely wild, rising to their flippers, cheering, ribbitting and screaming for all they were worth. It was the same in front of television sets across the world. Frogs and toads ribbitted themselves hoarse as this unknown frog, a trail of dust and sand in his wake, scampered across the beach toward the finish. He passed Foxy and closed in on Renco. With only a few metres to go he shut his eyes. He was hurting so much he could hardly bear it. Renco was almost at the line.

'I won't be second,' thought Todd. 'After all I've been through I will not be second.'

With a dozen or so huge strides, he passed Renco with only inches to spare, crashing over the finish line and falling to the ground in the biggest cloud of dust and sand.

He had won Superfrog.

17. One Month Later

'Hey Cleo, what do you call a frog with a paper bag on its head?'

'How should I know?'

'Russell!' said Boris.'

Cleopatra did not laugh.

'You know,' said Boris. 'Russell, as in rustle.'

'I know what you meant. It's just not funny.'

'I'd give up if I were you Boris,' laughed Todd.

The three frogs were at Jimmy's Frogjuice Bar and this was a celebration: the trial of Victor and Sly was over and Victor was locked up, in Frog City Prison, for a very long time.

Sly was not treated so harshly; although he had known about what his father had been doing he had not actually got involved; he was also in Frog City Prison, but for a much shorter period.

It turned out that the money Victor had ploughed into Plas Mega had been gained by fraudulent means. The judge, the honourable Lord Leapabout, ruled that everything Victor owned should be taken from him and given to the people of Frog City. The mansion was already being converted into an outdoor centre and the Frog City Police department were using Sly's helicopter for crime prevention.

Unfortunately for Frog City, Las Mega could not be treated in quite the same way; it was to be sold to the highest bidder (various rich entrepreneurs were already interested) and the money raised would be invested in a new school, a new marina and various other beneficial projects.

'How's your dad Todd?' asked Cleopatra.

'He's great,' said Todd. 'It's almost like everything that happened was a bad dream. He's back at work and very happy. Mum's her normal self as well, and she's got a job at the bakery. We paid the council the money we owed and I bought Mum and Dad a new car. Dad won't drive it; he's too stuck in his ways and won't take lessons. But Mum loves it; she's taking lessons. Dad says that she can be his driver. Anyway, I bought him a mountain-bike and he goes to work on it.'

'What about the new job,' asked Boris, 'when do you start?'

'I turned it down,' said Todd.

'What!' exclaimed Boris. 'You turned down a job with Frog TV? You must be mad.'

Todd laughed. 'I decided that I want to do something for Frog City. I don't quite know what yet, but when I look around I see so many things that could be improved. Anyway, I've got an interview tomorrow with Frog City Council, at the Tourism Office. I thought I could start there – if they'll have me.'

'That's great,' said Cleopatra. 'I think it's a wonderful idea.'

Boris sprinkled some bug's eyes on his garlic worms. 'Hey Todd, you might be Mayor of Frog City one day!'

Todd laughed. Now that was a crazy idea. One of those ideas that any normal frog might think about for only one second before dismissing it from his mind …

Time for Flight

The blackbird had enjoyed her summer at Frog Pond, but she will shortly have to journey south: the nights are drawing in and the leaves turning brown. She will return again next year.

The pond is quiet now that the tourists have gone. A few small boats zigzag across the water, but down at the waterfront the shops and restaurants are generally quiet.

It is dusk. Below the tree, close to the bank, something in the pond catches the blackbird's eye. Three dark shapes move silently through the water, their dorsal fins briefly exposed as they cross the shallows towards the lights of the city. They are not alone. In their wake are further shapes, too many to easily count, small, yet perfectly formed, and gliding as easily across the shallows as their larger kin. Soon they will leave their parents and explore the pond alone.

The blackbird feels the urge to take flight. She ruffles her feathers and prepares her wings. Something is wrong; there is danger on the wind. She takes flight.